# The Fireman's Flame

Meredith Green

Next Chapter Publishing—Leesburg, VA
ISBN: 978-0-692-18180-5
Library of Congress Control Number (Pending)
*The Fireman's Flame* | Meredith Green
Available Formats: eBook | Paperback distribution

# Dedication

To my own knight in shining armor -
Without you, this book would never have been written. Thank you for always pushing me to try harder, helping me to be a better person, and for your unending patience, unfailing strength, even your unyielding stubborn insistence that I do this...and above all, your unfounded but somehow unwavering faith in me. You will never know how much it means.

# Chapter 1

The oppressive, steamy heat of a late summer afternoon in New England sapped the strength of anyone unfortunate enough to be outside. Elizabeth Andrews was no exception. With a tired sigh, she stretched her neck against the knots that had been building up for ages.

Being a massage therapist, she would normally have been getting massages regularly. Things had been a bit insane for her lately and her own care had fallen by the wayside. Jake would fuss at her she knew, but there was nothing to be done about it now.

A genuine smile spread across her full lips as she thought of the man she called her best friend. Jacob Carpenter had been out of town for the last two days attending the birthday party of another friend. Now, his flight was due in any minute and she was still a half hour away. Not that he would be upset, she knew. It was just she'd missed him and really wanted to be there when he got back. He had asked her to go with him but, due to some prior plans, she was unable to.

Only a couple inches taller than her, he had a crooked little grin that could melt the bones of pretty much any woman he turned it on, herself included though she would never let him know that. His eyes, warm and brown, always reminded her of a cup of coffee with just a few drops of cream. They changed depending on his emotions though and she wondered if he even knew it. She knew him well enough now to read his moods just by looking at his eyes.

Though Jacob was by no means a bodybuilder, his body was definitely built. His hard work as a firefighter and paramedic, as well as the countless hours spent in the gym, saw to that. She would be hard pressed to think of anywhere that he had an ounce of body fat and she had looked plenty - before she'd gotten over her adolescent case of puppy love for him of course. Admittedly though, she still took a second look when he walked around without his shirt, which was pretty often during the warmer months. His broad shoulders and well-developed chest caught the eye of any red blooded female in sight and he knew it.

He kept his sandy brown hair cut short, but she liked it on him. The almost military style suited him somehow. He'd once made a comment about growing it out a little and had laughed outright at her horrified reaction.

All in all, he was a good looking man. Lean-hipped, and flat-bellied, he had a body most guys worked hard for and still didn't achieve. His strong jaw and hard mouth belied the gentleness she knew was an innate part of him. She also knew that that mouth wasn't as hard as it looked. She forced that thought away before it could finish forming.

She'd had a crush on him since she was a sophomore in high school, but liked to pretend she had gotten over it as time went on. Still, they were best friends and saw each other through everything. From deaths to weddings to divorces, they were side by side. Only one thing had ever threatened their relationship: Jake's ex-wife. Two things, she amended, but Jake didn't know about the other, and for now at least, that's how it would remain. Someday, she would have to tell him, but there seemed no point presently, and would only subject him to unnecessary pain.

When she was sixteen, Elizabeth's parents had been killed in a car accident. She had been an only child and there was no one else left for her. Because she had no family, the Carpenters had unofficially adopted her and treated her as if she was one of their own. Jake and his brothers harassed and picked on her as much as they would have their own sister, had they had one. His mother coddled and fussed over her like she was her own little girl and his father, just like he and his brothers, would quite happily tear apart anyone who dared to hurt her.

Elizabeth still remembered the time in high school that Jake and his brothers had "had words" with Jonathan, one of the guys in her chemistry class. Apparently the boy had been spreading dirty lies about Elizabeth and the boys had found out about it. Nobody had ever told Elizabeth what happened but Jake and both of his brothers had been suspended for three days each and the next time she'd seen Jonathan, he'd been sporting two black eyes and various other assorted bumps and bruises. He'd never dared to so much as look at her after that.

Brad and Laura Carpenter normally didn't condone their boys fighting and had been more than a little upset when they received the call from the school that day. However, when Jake and his brothers explained what had happened, their parents had backed their sons up without hesitation. Brad had even gone far enough to say it was better they had gotten hold of the boy than he.

Even in his late fifties, Brad was a man one

would be wise not to cross. He had spent twenty years in the army and had worked hard to maintain his physique. It had paid off and he could easily pass for ten years younger than he was. His crystal blue eyes were as sharp as ever and seemed to miss nothing. In spite of his slim form, his mind and heart were as large as ever and anyone who knew him knew they had a friend.

Laura Carpenter was also in her fifties but looked like she was in her late thirties at most, except for the silver hair. Her brown eyes had been passed on to two of her three sons, and were just as clear as theirs were. While she joked about needing to lose weight, she was not a large woman. And her heart was solid gold, as anyone would say.

His brothers, Nick and Logan, were something else. They had physical resemblance to both parents in some ways, but none of the three sons looked much like the other two. Even so, there was a bond there between them that couldn't be denied.

Nick was the same age as Elizabeth and was the carefree, prankster type. He had inherited more of his father's looks than his mother's. Tall and lean, he also had his father's blue eyes and keen sight. Nick was a police officer and a very respected one at that. He'd worked very hard at everything he did and it showed.

Logan was six years older than Elizabeth. He was by far the most serious in the entire family. When he was eighteen, Logan had joined the military and had been deployed a couple of times since Elizabeth had known them. The last deployment had been the hardest and Logan had never quite seemed the same. He'd been struggling with PTSD and had unwisely turned to alcohol at first to help numb the pain. Fortunately, good counseling and the love of his family had stopped things before they'd gone too far in that direction.

Traffic started moving finally, and Elizabeth breathed a sigh of relief. The air conditioning in her car was moody at best and, at the moment, was being mouthy about working. Even in New England, sitting still in the sun could quickly become pretty stifling.

Humidity from the unusually warm day had caused some of her curls to escape the French braid she had put them in that morning. The tendrils framed her face, clinging to her temples and she could feel trickles of sweat winding down between her breasts and soaking into her back. Now that traffic was moving, she hoped that the slight breeze would cool her off enough that she didn't look like she'd spent all day working out in the gym.

A few moments later, Elizabeth pulled into a parking space near the far end of the parking lot. She muttered under her breath about the walk ahead even though she had fully expected it when she'd spoken to Jake earlier and he'd told her when his plane would be arriving. A quick glance at her watch showed his plane should have touched down about fifteen minutes prior and she quickened her step even more.

Never one for heels, she was thankful she had worn her sneakers for this excursion as she all but ran across the pavement toward the large building. A short sleeved dark green scrub shirt topped matching scrub pants, and the color complimented her greenish blue eyes and dark auburn hair. She hadn't had time to change between work and coming to pick Jake up from the airport. Though she had confined her hair earlier in the best semblance of order she could manage, the locks still weighed heavily on her back as she stepped into the cool, darker interior of the terminal.

She paused for a moment, allowing her eyes to adjust to the comparatively dim light of the building. After getting her bearings, she headed to the nearest arrivals board and groaned to find that Jake's plane had landed on time. This meant that he was either at the baggage claim already, or wandering around the airport looking for her.

Though he was the sweetest man she'd ever met, he wasn't the most patient and had a tendency to get restless. She hoped that he'd had baggage to check this time although she doubted it. At least, if he did, he would be somewhere nearby. Otherwise, there was no telling where he could be.

Just as she was thinking that, she heard her name and turned. There he was. Her Jake. She knew he wasn't hers, but she'd always thought of him that way. They had both had their rough patches in life but had leaned on each other and made it through. Jake was four years her senior and, although Jake's younger brother Nick had actually been in Elizabeth's graduating class, they had never gotten as close as she and Jake had.

Elizabeth didn't believe in fairy tales, anymore. There was no such thing as happily ever after. In spite of that, she had always seen Jake as her own personal knight in shining armor. Whenever there was a problem, it was Jake who came to her rescue. He was forever saving her, just being there for her, or occasionally even giving her a good swift kick in the rear. Figuratively of course.

He always told her that if it wasn't for her, he wouldn't have made it through his divorce. She always denied it though and claimed it was his own stubbornness that had done it. Either way, she'd thought being there for him to be merely a small payment against all he and his family had done for her since the deaths of her parents.

Though his divorce had brought her the happiest night of her life, she knew it had come with a price. On the night of her eighteenth birthday, Jake had made love to her. She had known that it wasn't actually her he wanted, but she hadn't cared. Young and in love, she had all but thrown herself at him and been more than willing to deal with the consequences later. Little had she known that the results would impact her even now as she watched him walk toward her. Someday she would have to tell Jake, she thought, but not today.

Jake felt a huge grin split his face as he caught a glimpse of dark auburn hair. His Elizabeth was a one of a kind woman and that hair was as one of a kind as she was. Curling around her face as it was, combined with her figure, it attracted quite a bit of male attention. Jake noticed and felt an inexplicable shot of annoyance at the men following her with their eyes. Though he had no claim on her, he felt a strange twinge of possessiveness toward the woman he'd known for so long.

His smile seemed to both falter and widen at the same time. It was weird but it seemed much longer than two days since he'd seen her, and seeing her now made him more than a little happy. Having said that, however, his excitement was tempered by the growing number of men looking her way.

Not that he could blame them. Tilting his head slightly, he watched her approach. Her long, easy stride moved her toward him quickly, her hips swaying tantalizingly with each step. Though the scrubs she wore could hardly be considered sexy, they failed miserably to disguise the full extent of her appeal.

The unisex top couldn't conceal the full, lush curve of her high, round breasts. It did skim away from her slender belly and waist though, leaving at least that to the imagination. Scrub pants didn't exactly accentuate the curve of her hips and backside, but could hardly disguise them. Her long, lean legs made up most of her height, which was considerable for a woman. Although she was tall and had a broad shouldered build, there was no denying her femininity.

Within reach of each other at last, they embraced, hugging each other tight, and Jacob held on far longer than necessary, sending a silent but unmistakable message to the men who'd been eyeing Elizabeth. This time, their usual peck on the cheek wasn't enough for him and he brushed his lips lightly across hers. The caress was gone before it started, lasting just long enough to fluster Elizabeth and tint her cheeks a little more pink than they already were.

Somewhat bewildered by the unexpected show of affection, she stared at Jake for a moment. He hadn't kissed her even casually since that one night except on the cheek. To have him do so now surprised and baffled her.

Even more baffling was the feeling that it had been so much longer than two days that he'd been away. It seemed to her that it had been a week since she had seen his face. There was no doubt it was far more than a mere forty-eight hours since he had wrapped her in his arms and pulled her close in a goodbye hug.

It didn't matter, she told herself. Now, he was here with her again. Everything was as it should be. Well, almost everything.

Looping his arm around the slightly shorter Elizabeth, Jake grinned at her pink face and damp hair. She was more than a little warm. On top of that, she looked flustered and he had no doubt that traffic had been the main cause of it. She hated traffic and it was always bad at this time of day. He also knew him kissing her like that hadn't helped. Lord knew it had flustered him.

"Air conditioning out again?" he teased, tucking a stray curl behind her ear.

She rolled her eyes and nodded.

"Of course. I'm afraid it's going to be a long, hot ride home today," she announced regretfully.

Jake chuckled and shrugged.

"I've got a long, hot ride for you," he whispered suggestively so only she could hear.

Though they both knew he was kidding, Elizabeth's cheeks burned nonetheless. She knew perfectly well what he meant. Much as she wished she could deny it, the idea of taking him up on that was far too hard to resist.

From the corner of her eye, she saw the self-satisfied little grin on his face and knew he had succeeded in his goal. For some reason, he and his brothers seemed to take a perverse delight in making her blush. Sometimes they would even go out of their way to tell or retell particularly raunchy jokes around her, just for the reaction.

"Jake!" she protested without heat. "You're

horrible!"

"Yeah, but you love me anyway," he grinned.

He had no idea, she thought to herself.

Out loud, she said, "Yeah, that's why I'm going to roast you on the way home."

"That's ok. We'll just get all hot and sweaty together in your car," a grin still adorned his face as he dodged her playful elbow.

He loved picking on her and making comments like that because she always blushed so prettily. It amused him to know that she was still so innocent that she would blush at simple statements. Though lord only knew what, there was just something about the way she looked with her face so pink that always got to him. Perhaps it was the tantalizing thought of just how far down the color went, and the temptation to someday find out for himself.

His Elizabeth was something else. She had the quicksilver temper long associated with redheads, but just as quickly as she flared up, she was apologizing for it. A sweeter, gentler soul he'd never met, save his mother. She was loyal to a fault, and would do anything for anyone. He was a lucky man to have her in his life, he knew.

He was also very lucky she'd forgiven him for what had happened on her eighteenth birthday.

His brief lapse of control and judgment could have cost him her friendship. Fortunately, she'd born him no grudge over it. As he always did when thoughts of that night intruded on his consciousness, he ruthlessly shoved it aside. He concentrated instead on other thoughts of the woman at his side.

Her one fault was being unwilling to admit when she needed something. He couldn't count how many times things had happened in her life and she'd done her best to keep it to herself. He hadn't found out about her parents' deaths for three days and when he did, it wasn't from her.

His eyes darkened with the memory now. Nick had come home that day, clearly upset. As soon as he'd spotted Jake, he'd asked him to check on Elizabeth. She hadn't been to school that week and he was worried.

Jake had felt a sick knot tighten his gut. Earlier that week, some of the guys at the station had been talking about a double fatality accident they'd worked the night before. He had dismissed it at the time, not thinking any more of it than he normally did. Surely if Elizabeth or her parents had been involved, he'd have heard.

Still, the painful tightness in his stomach got worse when he called her cell and house and got no answer. He had taken the front steps two at a time and had backed his car out of the driveway before Nick made it to the front porch.

The drive had been completed in record time and he all but screeched to a halt in front of the familiar house. There were no vehicles in the driveway and if possible his chest tightened even more. He half ran to the door, praying he was wrong. The knob turned easily in his hand and the door opened into the darkened house.

A shiver ran down his spine as he realized how empty the house felt. He heard a small sound, almost indiscernible, from the back of the house and cleared the length of the hallway in about a second. The noise had come from Elizabeth's room and he raised his hand to knock before realizing the door was cracked.

Elizabeth lay on her bed, silent and unmoving. Her features were ashen, her eyes dull and dark. She stared at a picture frame on her bedside table, but he knew she didn't see it. The late afternoon light wasn't enough to illuminate her room beyond the bare minimum, but he didn't want to risk startling her by turning on her light.

Instead, he slowly pushed the door open and eased into the room. The girl on the bed didn't move. She didn't even know he was there.

Softly, he spoke her name. Only then did she show any signs of life, and only barely. Her eyes moved from the tormenting image of the photo in front of her to the man now standing beside her bed. They were still dull and unfocused and he wondered if she even realized he was there.

She spoke at last, her voice barely a whisper, "They're gone, Jake."

The words were so heart wrenching that Jake could barely stand it. That was what he'd feared. He nodded silently and took another step closer.

"I know, babe."

She pushed herself upright until she was sitting on the edge of the bed and he sat beside her. Neither of them spoke for long moments, neither sure what to say. Jake knew he should say or do something, but knew there were no words for the pain the girl felt at that moment.

He didn't touch her, afraid if he did she would break. The tension within her was palpable and he could feel her battle for control. She would lose. He knew that. But, he wouldn't be the reason. He would be there and hold her when she fell apart, but he wouldn't be the instrument to undo her.

Then the storm broke. It started softly with a couple of shaky breaths and he knew it was over. He pulled her across his lap and held her while she sobbed uncontrollably. Rocking silently, his heart ached for her and he wished he could ease her pain.

They stayed like that for hours. Long after her tears had subsided, he held her, rocking and gently stroking her hair. She clung to him, holding on for dear life.

He knew the memory of that night would never fade. Even all these years later, it still hurt to remember her pain. There were other nights he would never forget either, but that was the night that had ultimately changed the course of their lives forever.

From that night on, Elizabeth had all but moved in with the Carpenters. The state had put her in a foster home since she was sixteen already but Jake's mother had spoken to the authorities multiple times about having her live with them. Due to overloading the girl had fallen through the cracks in the system. Always citing one reason or another and producing endless paperwork, they had denied Laura's requests to have Elizabeth move in with the only people she had left. It had ultimately been a moot point as she only spent her nights at the foster home. Every waking moment that she wasn't in school, she was with the Carpenters.

Except when she'd inexplicably and suddenly decided to go traveling for a few weeks, immediately after graduation, they'd never gone more than a few days without seeing each other. He'd tutored her in physics and calculus her senior year, helping her pull her dwindling grades to straight A's. She was very smart and had been a very attentive study, even if half the time he'd found himself distracted by her. It was safe to say that immediate family aside, Elizabeth was the biggest constant in his life. Even his ex-wife's presence hadn't lasted more than a couple years in his life, total.

When he'd married Sharon, Elizabeth had just turned seventeen. He'd been twenty-one and bound and determined that Sharon was the one for him. Elizabeth had been less willing to buy into it and had been very reserved around Sharon.

Jake had been oblivious to the tension between the two women. Sharon had been everything he'd ever wanted, or so he told himself. Tall, blond and lean, her blue eyes were clear and bright. He'd had no clue what was to come.

Less than a year later, when his marriage was breaking up Elizabeth had been different around him, guarded somehow. She was still there for him and was still as supportive as ever, but she wasn't Elizabeth. The joking that always accompanied their conversation was notably absent. He would find her sullen and staring at nothing and when he asked what was wrong, she forced a painful semblance of a smile and assured him she was fine. It went on for several weeks, till he could stand it no longer.

Finally, he'd cornered her and demanded that she tell him what was wrong. Stubbornly, she'd refused, and turned to walk away from him. He'd turned her back around, forcing her to meet his gaze and was shocked at the sadness in her eyes. Then, there was no way he was letting her go till she told him. She had resisted still, saying she couldn't tell him and begging him not to make her. Her pleas left him unmoved and, eventually, she bowed her head admitting defeat.

"I should have stopped this. I never trusted her. I didn't know why. There was just something about her that I never trusted. I don't know why and I can't explain it. Then, not long before your wedding, I saw her in town with Joe."

Joe was the local bad-boy and had a reputation for changing women more than he did his clothes. His fascination with Sharon had been short lived, but it was enough for Elizabeth to still hate them both for what they had done to Jake. He deserved better than that.

"I confronted her of course, telling her that she needed to come clean with you. Or I would."

She laughed bitterly at the memory. The older woman had shown her true nature and then some when threatened with having the truth revealed to her fiancé. Sharon's mouth had twisted in a sneer as she pointed out that she had Jake wrapped so tightly around her finger he would believe anything she told him. She had taken great pleasure in assuring Elizabeth that if she breathed one word of what she'd seen, then not only would she see to it that her friendship with Jake came to an abrupt and painful end, but also that Jake would be hurt.

"She said all she would have to do is deny it and tell you I was jealous. You would believe her and think I was just trying to take you away from her. Then, you would have nothing to do with me ever again. I would've dealt with that. It would have killed me but I would have done even that to keep you from being hurt. But then she pointed out that, if I was the one who told, then I was the one who would be responsible for breaking your heart. She said that if you didn't know it wasn't going to hurt you. That it meant nothing anyway and that there was no point breaking your heart over it. I knew better than to believe that it meant nothing but I couldn't stand the thought of being the one to hurt you. I should have known better."

Jake had stared at her stunned, releasing her in disbelief. He had known Sharon was capable of being vengeful and spiteful, but he'd had no idea of the true depths of her cruelty. As much as he wanted to deny it, he knew his ex-wife was right. He would have believed her. Although there was no way in hell she would have ended his friendship with Elizabeth.

The lengths Sharon had gone through to manipulate Elizabeth into keeping her secret, though, shocked him. He knew that without that bit about being the one to hurt him, Elizabeth would indeed have followed through on her threat and told him exactly what she'd seen in order to protect him. What killed him was that Sharon had known that too and used it to deceive everyone.

Looking over at Elizabeth now, as she climbed into the driver's seat, Jake was struck anew with her strength and beauty. It was something he always did his best to ignore. He knew she wasn't the kind of girl he should be with. He would only end up hurting her. She was a sweet innocent girl and he was a hard cynical man. He loved her and had for a long time. But he'd shielded himself well against being *in* love with her, forcing himself to see her as a kid sister.

She made it hard sometimes, crawling under his skin as she did. Sometimes it seemed that the harder he tried to keep her out, the easier she slipped in. There were times, when the breeze carried her subtle sweet scent to him in the evenings they spent together, that it was tempting to see where they could go. When the moon reflected something dangerous and wonderful in her emerald eyes just right, it took every ounce of willpower he possessed to not take her in his arms and kiss her breathless, the way he wanted to.

Every time that urge hit him, he would force himself to remember Sharon and her betrayal. Ever since his divorce, he had had nothing but the most superficial relationships. He enjoyed the company of women, the physical side of the relationships, but kept his heart well out of harm's way. Somehow, with Elizabeth though, it was so much more difficult.

In his heart, he knew that Elizabeth was not the same kind of woman as his ex-wife. Elizabeth would never lie to him or hurt him the way Sharon had. Perhaps that was why he was so afraid of her.

His mind drifted as she drove and he recalled what had happened almost eight years ago. It had been Elizabeth's eighteenth birthday and his mother had thrown a big party for her, inviting everyone around. Unfortunately, Sharon had also been there at the restaurant with her new fiancé and trouble had ensued. Not content to merely be there and get along, Sharon had felt the need to flaunt her engagement, as well as the fact that after only four months, she was pregnant and it wasn't Jake's.

They had tried unsuccessfully for a baby the entire time they were together. Sharon had been impatient about conceiving, almost desperate in fact. Sometimes, looking back, Jake wondered if it was desperation to tie him to her permanently, to make sure he could never leave. Either way, she was pregnant and gloating about it and everyone noticed.

Jake had ignored Sharon as long as he could, which was no easy feat. It had seemed that the more he pretended she wasn't there, the harder she tried to goad him. She hung all over her fiancé, who didn't seem to mind at all, all but making out with the handsome blond in front of everyone there. The final straw had been when she pointed out quite loudly that Jake had been unable to get her pregnant the entire time they were together and questioned his "manhood."

Furious, Jake had stormed out and, after

finally letting loose and giving the older woman a blistering tirade that was still talked about occasionally, Elizabeth had gone after him. She'd found him sitting alone on the riverbank. Tucking her knees under her chin, she'd sat beside him, just giving him company for a while, then listening as he ranted and raved about the way his future ex-wife had been acting.

Pacing angrily, he'd occasionally hurled stones into the water in an attempt to work out some of the fury burning through him. She was pretty sure that some of the tosses would have rivaled a major league pitcher, though she knew he would not appreciate the comparison. Quietly, she waited while he yelled and swore and stalked back and forth in front of her.

Agreeing completely with his assessments of the woman's behavior, Elizabeth had sympathized with him. Then, having burned out all the anger he'd felt, Jake had dropped back beside Elizabeth, despondent. Instinctively, she'd hugged him tight while he blamed himself for the breakup. Somehow, he should have prevented it. He wasn't good enough, or attractive enough, or he'd been a bad husband. Elizabeth had known all of that wasn't true and had wanted to show him.

Unable to stop herself, she'd pressed her lips

to his. She'd intended the kiss only as comfort he knew, but had been helpless to control the reaction within him at the touch of her mouth on his. He'd kissed her back and pulled her closer, feeling her soft, feminine curves against him and that had been the end of his control.

# Chapter 2

Elizabeth pulled to a stop in front of Jake's apartment building, not remembering anything of the drive from the airport. She'd been lost in the past and hoped it hadn't been too obvious. From Jake's continued silence and distant look, she suspected he was just as lost as she had been. She wondered if he was thinking about the same thing she had been. His kiss at the airport, though brief, had brought the feelings of that night flooding back.

Suddenly, she realized he was staring at her and uncomfortably tucked a lock of hair behind her ear. He blinked and his eyes refocused as if he was waking from a dream and he realized that they were home. As he reached for the car door handle, he invited her in for a cold drink before she headed back to her own apartment.

She accepted and they walked companionably through the rapidly diminishing twilight. The air was still hot and Elizabeth couldn't wait to get home and take a nice long shower, but couldn't waste the opportunity to spend time with Jake when he'd been gone so long. She'd never admit it to him, but she got so lonely sometimes, and being with him always made her feel better.

He held the door open for her after unlocking it, allowing her to enter first as he always did. If nothing else, Jake was one of the few remaining gentlemen in the world, always treating women with deference and respect. Even if they didn't deserve it.

In the kitchen, they worked together silently, Jake retrieving glasses while Elizabeth grabbed a carton of lemonade from the refrigerator. The cool, tart liquid was refreshing and it was all Elizabeth could do not to trail the cool glass down her heated cheeks and over her throat. As it was, she held the frosty surface to her skin, tipping her head back and relishing the pleasant coolness.

Jake watched, transfixed, as Elizabeth's eyes drifted closed. Her lips parted slightly and he had one hell of a time trying not to lean over and kiss them. He knew she wasn't doing it on purpose, but damn the woman was driving him out of his mind.

Thankfully, she opened her eyes and once more lifted the drink to her lips. She took a small sip of the beverage, licking her lips after lowering the container to the countertop. Rolling her head on her shoulders to stretch her neck, she noticed boxes all over Jake's living room.

"Hey! What's going on?" she asked, confused.

She couldn't deny feeling a little stung that he'd not mentioned anything to her about moving. But there wasn't really another explanation for all the boxes stacked in the adjacent room.

"Oh!" he exclaimed, suitably distracted from her unintentional seduction a moment ago.

"It was going to be a surprise," he admitted sheepishly. "I signed the lease on a new apartment before I left the other day. Will be moving a little closer to you, actually."

"Oh?" she forgave the slip in not telling her, in favor of finding out how much closer he was going to be.

"Yeah, the apartment next door to you in fact."

She couldn't have been more shocked if she'd tried. Then, she laughed.

"Why don't you just move in with me and save the rent?" she joked without thinking.

Jake froze. The thought of being in the same apartment with her was enough to scare him to death. He already had one hell of a time trying not to touch her. No way he'd succeed if they were in the same household.

"Hey...earth to Jake," she teased.

He looked at her questioningly and she grinned.

"Relax. I was just kidding. Can you imagine us living together? We'd drive each other nuts!"

Well, he would certainly be insane before a week was done, he knew. Being around her while she did personal things, like showering, getting ready for bed, getting dressed in the mornings. His body reacted to the thought and he swore silently. Yeah, he'd be out of his mind in no time.

"Do you need some help moving?" she offered.

"Sure," he agreed gruffly, his mind not quite off the wayward thoughts he'd just had. "The guys are busy but may show up for the heavier lifting. But could definitely use help packing and moving the smaller stuff."

"Okay, tell me when and I'll be here," she stated as she drained the contents of her glass and rinsed it out before placing it in the dishwasher.

That was typical of her, he thought. She was always the first to offer help and always the last to ask for it. Stubborn, was what he called it. She preferred to refer to it as independent. Either way, she was as hard-headed as a mule.

Shaking his head with a grin, he told her it

would be about a month and she nodded, stifling a yawn. It had been a long day for her as she'd been at work before her drive to the airport to pick him up. Bed sounded really good to her at that moment and she reached up to give him a big hug before leaving.

Jake wrapped his arms around Elizabeth, enjoying the comfortable feel of her embrace. She kissed his cheek and murmured that she'd see him Saturday, if not before and he nodded, still holding her loosely. He wasn't willing to let her go just yet.

When he still didn't release her, Elizabeth looked up at him inquiringly. There was something hot and dangerous deep in his stare and her breath caught. Her heart felt as if it were going to leap out of her chest as his gaze moved to her mouth. Involuntarily, her tongue darted out to moisten her suddenly dry lips.

Jake's eyes darkened to the color of hot black coffee and Elizabeth swallowed hard, finding it suddenly difficult to breathe. She knew he was going to kiss her. His face moved closer with agonizing slowness until at last their mouths met.

His lips slid lazily across her own as his hand slid up to cup her cheek. Their mouths explored and relearned each other unhurriedly, taking their time as one kiss led to another. His fingers wound themselves into her hair, curling against her scalp. Gently tugging, he urged her head back exposing the long column of her neck.

Slowly, but with increasing hunger, his mouth traced a line of kisses down her jaw line and toward her collarbone. A soft moan escaped her and he encouraged it, nibbling his way back up the trail he'd just branded with his kisses until their mouths met once more. Her arms wound around his neck as she pulled him nearer.

With a low groan, he turned and backed her up against the refrigerator, pulling her closer as he did. God, she was sweet, he thought. The cool tang of the lemonade they had shared lingered on her lips and in the depths of her mouth, tempting him and teasing him. Her arms tightened around him, beckoning him even closer, though it didn't seem possible. The only way to be closer was to be inside her.

A bolt of electricity shot through him at the thought and suddenly he pulled away, panting as if he'd just run a mile. Elizabeth stared at him, her face flushed and her lips swollen from his kiss. Damn, he wanted to kiss her again. Her eyes were huge and green, sparks of passion shooting at him from deep within them.

He turned away before she noticed his

obvious arousal. It would be only too clear if she happened to look. The deep breaths he took, attempting to clear his head, did little to help. He could still smell her. The subtle scent of vanilla and citrus teased and tempted him, beckoning him back to her arms, calling him to bury his face in her neck and inhale the fragrance that was hers alone. Her hotly glowing eyes made him yearn to take her once more, to make her his again.

Swearing to himself again, he drew a ragged breath and counted to ten. Forcing himself to think about anything that would calm his raging hormones, he wondered at the reaction she could provoke in him. A simple kiss and he was so hard it hurt. Even Sharon had never done that to him. Only Elizabeth inspired this sort of turmoil. She had done it last time and again just now.

At last, he turned around to face her once more, slightly more composed than he had been mere seconds ago. She had unbraided her hair on the way to the car at the airport, opting instead for a messy bun that kept the heavy tresses off her neck. Now, she released them momentarily before gathering them once more and pulling them ruthlessly tight as she restrained them in the same manner. She did that when she was upset. Hell, was she upset about him kissing her? Probably.

He sighed and uttered an apology, surprised when she frowned at him. Women! They made no sense. She got upset because he'd kissed her then frowned when he apologized for it. There was no winning with them.

Her hair now properly in place once more, Elizabeth pushed herself away from the refrigerator, and started making her way to the door. She muttered something about seeing him later and all but ran for the front of his apartment. Damn, he hadn't meant to scare her off. Obviously he had though.

He warred with himself on whether or not to follow her and, in the end, decided not to. He'd probably only make things worse. She would cool off and things would be ok again.

Elizabeth knew he'd wanted her. His hardness against her had been proof enough of that. Heaven only knew why he'd stopped and furthermore why in the hell he'd apologized.

She fumed as she stalked to her car. He'd apologized to her. For kissing her! He'd done that the night they'd made love, too. Apparently, making love to her and kissing her were bad things to do. Men! They could be so dense sometimes!

Still practically steaming, she stopped beside her car to dig in her pocket for her keys. A quick pat down of all pockets revealed what she had feared and she swore long and low. She had left her keys on Jake's counter. Thankful for the second time that she had worn her sneakers, she turned on her heel and started walking.

He'd probably call her childish for it, and chew her out for walking home, but she'd be damned if she was about to go back up there and ask him for her keys. No way in hell. She raised her chin and quickened her pace.

Back at the apartment, Jake was cursing himself ten kinds of a fool. To be honest, he wasn't sure if it was for kissing her or for something else. He wasn't entirely sure what the hell had set her off in the first place. It ultimately didn't matter he knew, because either way she was pissed at him now. He sighed and turned to rinse his glass in the sink when his eyes fell on something shiny. Elizabeth's keys. She'd left them here.

A small chuckle escaped as he realized how mad she'd be about that one. Already being pissed at him, having to swallow her pride and come back for the keys would no doubt have her fit to be tied. He wondered if he should walk them down to her or wait for her to come back.

After only a second of hesitation, he snatched up his keys and hers, before heading out the door. He took the stairs two at a time down toward the parking lot. The streetlight reflected off her empty vehicle as he approached and his heart did a sick little flip in his chest as he scanned the area for any sign of her.

It only took an instant to decide she was nowhere in sight. Quickly he grabbed his cell, calling her and praying she would answer. Four rings and her soft, faintly drawled voice came on the voice mail greeting. The air turned blue as he let loose with a string of curses that would have had his mother washing his mouth out with soap even at his age.

He searched once more looking for any clue as to where she'd disappeared to. She was, he knew, just boneheaded enough to take off walking rather than come back and get her keys. A faint smile crossed his lips as he realized that she would get all the way home and be locked out.

His key scraped in the lock as he unlocked his truck and climbed inside. It wouldn't take him long to catch up to her with the truck he knew and he was right. He had just barely exited the apartment complex when he caught sight of her slender form picking its way over the loose gravel that littered the side of the pavement.

Applying the brake lightly, he lowered the passenger window and called out to her. At first, he thought she was going to ignore him and keep walking. For a moment, she did. Then he called to her again and she stopped abruptly.

It was odd he thought as her gaze met his, she looked sixteen again, standing there like that. Her arms were crossed over her chest, her expression indignant but hurt. If he didn't know better, he would swear she was still that young girl she'd been so many years ago.

The cloudless sky allowed the full moon to shine down on her like a spotlight. Her pale skin fairly glowed and her eyes gleamed hotly in the darkness. He could almost feel the angry vibration of her body.

Shaking himself back to the present, Jake stopped the truck beside her. He held up the keys that she'd left behind and remained silent. A silent war waged within her and he watched as she battled between pride and common sense. Common sense won out eventually, when he pointed out that she wouldn't be able to get in the apartment without the keys.

Her lips tightening, she walked to the truck and opened the passenger door, intending to grab the keys and walk back to her car. Instead, he pulled the keys out of reach, insisting that it was just plain silly to walk back when he had to go back anyway. A frown greeted his statement and he knew he'd won again.

With obvious reluctance, she clambered into the vehicle, slamming the door with more force than necessary. She pulled the safety belt across her body clicking it into place and snatched the keys from Jake's hand, pulling herself as far to the opposite side of the confined space as she could. The soft sound of his chuckle in the darkness infuriated her even more. Damn it, he was laughing at her!

The more she tried to ignore him, the harder he laughed until she was positively boiling with rage. Finally, she could stand it no more.

"What the hell is so damn funny?" she snapped.

"Sorry, honey," he managed between full throated laughs, "but you are. You're so stubborn and you get so pissed off that you can't even think straight. And we both know five minutes later you're apologizing for it."

If she could have spit, she would have. The man was *mocking* her! Fortunately for him, she was not a violent woman, because the temptation to smack him right upside his smug little head was great at the moment.

He guided the truck back into the parking space he'd left only moments before and killed the engine. Pausing for a moment, he just looked at her. Damned if he knew what he'd done to make her so mad, but he did feel bad and wished he could make it better.

Given a day or two, she'd be over whatever it was whether he apologized or not. But somehow that wasn't good enough. He wanted them to be ok tonight.

Silently, he reached for her hand across the faintly moonlit cab of his truck. His large hand covered her much smaller one and he squeezed lightly till she looked at him. She had already calmed down a lot, he could tell, but was still visibly upset.

"Hey, listen honey. Whatever I did up there that upset you, I'm sorry. If it was the kiss-"

Elizabeth's features tightened and she pulled her hand away. Immediately, she missed the warmth of his palm covering her hand. But she couldn't think clearly when he was touching her like that.

"It wasn't," she denied stiffly.

"Well then, what-?" he started to ask.

"It's nothing Jake," she answered tightly. "Don't worry about it."

"But I-"

"Look, just chalk it up to hormones or whatever, ok? I'll be fine."

It was Jake's turn to sigh and he drummed his fingers against the steering wheel trying to figure out what the hell to do now. The damned woman wouldn't even let him apologize to her or tell him what he'd done wrong in the first place. And why did he even care? She'd forgive him by morning anyway. They both knew that. Still, something didn't feel right and he felt compelled to try to make it better.

"I'm sorry I laughed at you," he murmured softly, drawing a stunned look from her.

Over the years, he had laughed with her, at her and about her. Never once had he apologized for it. There had never been a need. She had always known there was no cruel intent behind it. But now he was apologizing to her. Maybe he really was just trying to make things right between them. Perhaps she was being too hard on him.

After all, she knew what a man of honor he was. Knowing him, in his mind, it was somehow taking advantage of her to kiss her. She wished she knew for sure. Maybe someday she would. And when she did find out, if that was the reason for it, she was going to take his "honor" and stick it somewhere very unpleasant for him.

For now, she heaved another sigh and shrugged her shoulders. Better to just forgive him now. She couldn't stand the thought of going home for the night with him upset, or thinking she was upset with him. They had rarely ever fought and she didn't want to start now.

"It's ok. I guess it was pretty ridiculous to go walking home just because I didn't want to come ask you for my keys."

"A little," he conceded cautiously.

"And you're right. I would have been screwed when I got home and couldn't get in. The office is closed so I'd have been stuck outside all night."

"Unless you called me," he pointed out softly.

She chuckled and rolled her eyes at the suggestion.

"Oh yeah, that would have gone well," she agreed sarcastically, then mimed holding a phone to her ear. "Um, hey Jake? Remember how I stormed out of your place a little bit ago? Well I left my keys and I'm at home now. Can you bring me my keys please?"

He laughed a little in response.

"True. Boy, you'd have really been pissed then," he agreed.

"Probably wouldn't have spoken to you for another two days," she added, cracking a smile.

"Oh at least," he smirked. "Good thing I was a gentleman and brought you your keys instead of making you do that, hmm?"

"First time for everything," she retorted.

"Yeah well don't get used to it, lady," he grinned.

Reluctantly, he turned to get out of the truck so she could go home.

Elizabeth waited for Jake to come around and open her door, having learned from years of experience that doing so herself would earn her nothing but a dirty look for her trouble. Sometimes she did it anyway, just to get a reaction but this time she was willing to let him play gentleman. As he held the door open, she slid out and into his arms. He held her close for a moment as she returned his embrace.

A smile of pure contentment slowly faded as she realized that she was thinking thoughts that she shouldn't be. Again. She was thinking how nice it would be to have this happen all the time, to come home from an evening out and slip into his arms just like this and have him holding her close enough that she could feel his breath on her ear, feel his heartbeat.

Slowly and reluctantly, she pulled away,

kissing his cheek lightly and turned to walk to her car. He watched for a moment before he called out to her to text or call when she got home.

A sassy little grin accompanied her mischievous, "We'll see," as she continued walking.

His hand snagged a belt loop on her jeans, halting her progress for a brief moment before she turned back to face him. She found his gaze unusually serious and intent as he took a step closer.

"Promise me," he murmured quietly.

Not sure what had prompted the intensity behind his request, she nodded once before whispering her agreement. Without a word, his lips brushed hers and he released her and stepped back. It was a moment before Elizabeth realized he'd let her go and she turned once more to make her way to her car.

# Chapter 3

The sunlight streaming in through Elizabeth's window awakened her far too early the next morning and she groaned as she cursed the brightness silently. If she didn't have clients scheduled for the day, she would just roll over and go back to sleep. Unfortunately, being a massage therapist meant that if she didn't work she didn't get paid. And not getting paid was a very bad thing.

If it was only herself, she might have considered going back to sleep anyway and just rescheduled the clients, but there were her employees to think of too. Lexi and Katie relied on her for their income. Lexi was the new therapist she had recently hired and Katie, or Katelyn, had been her receptionist for the last several months.

It was only about an hour later when, coffee in hand, Elizabeth unlocked the front door to the office that housed one of the few massage clinics in the area. Not having many other places around afforded her the comfort of knowing she had little competition. The ones that were there were only the same size or smaller than her own.

She had never really done much advertising but had found that word of mouth brought in a lot of business. There had been countless clients who had walked through the door she passed through at that moment, who had come because a friend or coworker had highly recommended her.

Her professionalism, combined with her friendly compassionate approach, set even the most anxious of clients at ease. It hadn't taken long before she found herself consistently booked for full days. What normally took a therapist two years to do, she had achieved in a short eight months.

With a deep sigh of pride, Elizabeth took a quick look around at the business she had built herself. She never could have done it, never *would* have done it, without Jake and his family. Especially Jake. They had supported her, pestered her and pushed her. He had nagged and pressed her even more, making her keep going when she wanted to quit. Their faith in her abilities had never wavered, even when her own had seemed to be gone for good.

Now, failure was not an option. After all they had done for her, and all they continued to do, she couldn't fail. She couldn't bear the thought of letting them all down.

A small, cruel voice in the back of her head whispered that she had done so in the weeks following her eighteenth birthday. Not to mention, every day since then. Brutally, she shut the voice out, moving through the waiting area toward her actual office.

The building was small, making it perfect for a private practice such as Elizabeth's. Jake had actually been the one to find it. It was directly across the street from the fire department and his parents' house. Elizabeth had been concerned initially about the proximity to the station, given that the sirens might disturb her clients. With the right soundproofing though, it had worked splendidly.

Looking at it now, she couldn't have asked for a better location, or a better setup. Walking in the door, one came into the waiting and reception room. Four large, comfortable looking chairs sat against the walls, allowing a relaxing place to sit while waiting for appointments.

Off the waiting room was a short hallway leading to the treatment rooms, Elizabeth's office, bathrooms, and a small kitchen where she and her employees could take time to sit down and enjoy a meal on their breaks. Admittedly though, more often than not, Elizabeth would eat in her office if she ate at all. Sometimes, Jacob would come over and bring her food, and they would eat together in the small room.

Much like her apartment, Elizabeth's office wasn't anything fancy. The wall behind her desk displayed her high school diploma, massage school diploma, state license and various other certificates proudly proclaiming her level of expertise. There was a small plant in the window behind her chair as well. The only picture she had in the room was a modest sized photo of Jake and his family.

They had been the ones who insisted that she needed more than just her certificates on her walls so she had a couple of portraits to prevent the ivory walls from being too sterile. The glossy pine floors gave the small room a touch of elegance without being too overbearing. A large area rug added a bit of color and practicality, cushioning the floor and preventing sounds from echoing.

From her desk, Elizabeth could see the front door and an open doorway allowed her to see the front desk as well. The view was ideal, allowing her to see almost the entire waiting room from where she sat. It made it much easier to ensure that no client was left waiting because their arrival had been unnoticed.

After starting up her computer, Elizabeth made her way down the hallway to the kitchen. She knew both of her employees thrived on coffee in the morning and she always tried to ensure that there was some freshly made when they arrived. That done, she headed back to her desk to take a look at her email and check the appointments for the day.

She sat down and started up the internet, gazing across the street as she waited for the page to load. Sometimes, her internet service was really good and things would load instantly. Other times, it seemed to take forever.

A small, silly smile spread across her face as she found herself thinking about Jake again. God, she needed to stop that. Katie would be in shortly and Lexi would follow soon after. All she needed was for them to catch her daydreaming like an idiot. Katie was already convinced that there was more between her and Jake than met the eye. The last thing that needed to happen was for her to catch Elizabeth mooning over him. Again.

Elizabeth smiled to herself. Katie was a sweet girl. Nick had actually met her first. He had pulled her over for speeding the night she came into town. She had been in a bad situation was all Nick would say when he had asked Elizabeth to give the girl a job.

She shuddered as she remembered now how bad the "situation" had been. The ensuing events had rocked this small town to its core. Never before, or since, had there been such horrid and terrifying events within its own borders. It was surely divine providence that Nick had been the one Katie met upon arriving here for, in the end, they had saved each other's lives, literally.

After hearing her story, Elizabeth had had no choice but to hire the young woman. Not once had she regretted the decision. Katie was a dedicated employee and went out of her way to help around the office in any way she possibly could.

The outer door opened and Elizabeth looked up from her desk to find the subject of her thoughts arriving for work. They greeted each other and Katie reached over to turn on the "open" sign before placing her things on the floor behind the desk.

With only a little bit of good-natured envy, Elizabeth looked once more at the younger woman. A petite blond, with the bluest eyes she had ever seen, Katie was the kind of girl who could have easily been a supermodel. Elizabeth had told her that once only to have her laugh it off as impossible. Besides, Katie had pointed out, there was no way she would leave Nick and the children for that long.

She smiled as her thoughts drifted back through time. Katie and Nick had only known each other for a few months when Nick proposed. Initially, Katie had rejected him. Nobody, not even Nick, had blamed the gun-shy young lady. But eventually with persistence, and of course the small matter of saving her and her son, Katie's resistance fell and she had agreed to become Nick's wife. The wedding was in a few short weeks. Elizabeth was going to be her maid of honor.

Katie and Nick had agreed that, after the wedding, Nick would adopt her son Tyler. The wedding had originally been planned for six months previous, but an unexpected gift had delayed events a little. Katie had become pregnant and they both agreed they didn't want to have the wedding till the baby was born.

The little girl, Evie, had been born just a few months ago and had her mother's fair coloring and her daddy's bright blue eyes. The small family had overcome seemingly insurmountable obstacles to be together. Even now, it was more than obvious any time Katie and Nick were in the same room that they were madly in love with each other

Forcing her thoughts back to the present, Elizabeth moved the mouse on her desk to open her appointment software. Her first client should be arriving shortly and she wanted to have a look at the chart before they did. The good thing with having so many regular clients was that eventually, she could recall pretty much everything she needed to know just by seeing the name. Still, she preferred to at least glance at the history each time.

Through the window, she watched a familiar truck pull into the fire station across the street. Jake's long lean frame unfolded from the vehicle and he glanced over her way before disappearing into the brick building that was a central part of their small town. Seeing him again, her thoughts wandered helplessly again to that long ago night.

After they had made love, Elizabeth lay there, trembling but ecstatic with the knowledge of what had just happened. The cool night air didn't seem so cool in the heated aftermath of their joining. After a long moment, Jake sat up and buried his face in his hands.

When he had said nothing, Elizabeth had sat up as well, pulling his shirt up to cover herself. She had touched his shoulder gently, wondering what to say. Then he had apologized. He had given her the most beautiful moments of her life, and he was apologizing.

He had given her some speech about her being young and innocent. Something had been mentioned about him taking advantage of her. He'd told her it hadn't been right for him to do what he'd done because he didn't love her, not that way, and never could. She couldn't remember it all, but she recalled enough to know he had regretted what they'd done. Immediately. He hadn't even waited till the next day, or the next week.

The outer door opened again, drawing Elizabeth from her reverie and she yanked her mind back to the business at hand. Her first client was here and it was time to begin her day. There would be time enough later for her to dwell on what might have been.

A few hours later, Jake stood in the lobby of Elizabeth's small massage clinic. He occasionally came over to see if she had time to work on him. Most of the time, she didn't. Business was good and he was glad of that. He was very proud of what she'd done on her own.

When she didn't have time on her schedule, she would usually stay late just for him. He always tried to pay her and she always refused, telling him that she didn't charge family.

Fortunately for his conscience though, she normally did allow him to take her to dinner afterward.

Right now, though, Elizabeth was in session and he chatted amicably with his soon to be sister-in-law. From her, he found out it would be about five more minutes before she was finished with her client. She didn't have any availability during normal office hours for the day, but Katie promised to leave a note for Elizabeth to call him and let him know if she could fit him in after hours.

While he waited, Jake took in the cozy but spacious lobby he and his family had helped her decorate. He smiled at the memory. Elizabeth had insisted on buying everyone pizza, beer and sodas that day and everyone had come to help. His brothers, their parents, and of course Jake himself had spent the entire day painting and arranging furniture.

They had hung a few paintings on the wall, too, including one special one they had bought for her as a congratulations on her new practice. It wasn't anything dramatic, just a seascape with a multicolored sunset in the background. The artwork seemed to draw the room together and Elizabeth had insisted on giving it a place of honor, right in the center of the wall opposite the door. It was the first thing that one noticed upon entering the small room.

The walls had been painted a pinkish-orange color that Elizabeth had insisted was called smoked salmon. To him, it just looked pink...or orange...he was never quite sure which. Either way the overall effect of the color, combined with the artwork and strategic lighting, was one that produced a feeling of well-being and peace. He guessed that was essential and desirable when one was working in this field.

The floor was a muted gray carpet with occasional flecks of the same "salmon" color that covered the walls. Elizabeth had debated having hardwood but decided against it upon further consideration. She had decided that it might be too distracting to clients relaxing in session if a new client came in with heels or boots, echoing on a wooden floor.

Katie finished writing and stuck the note on the top of the computer screen where she was certain Elizabeth couldn't miss it. With a smile, she told Jake Elizabeth should be calling or texting him shortly and asked if he was sure he didn't want to wait. Tempting as it was to wait and see Elizabeth for himself, he knew he really should get back across the street to work. He'd only snuck out for a couple minutes and needed to be there in case they received a call.

He was just turning away from the desk when they heard one of the doors in the back close, signaling the end of the session Elizabeth had been completing. Seconds later, she appeared and Jake smiled as she entered the room. She looked tired but still beautiful.

They embraced briefly and Katie hid a smile. She'd always thought the two of them belonged together. Elizabeth had vehemently denied that that was even a remote possibility the one time she had dared voice her thoughts on the matter, so she'd kept her mouth shut since then. Even she could see the chemistry between them though, and she silently harbored the hope that one day they would realize it for themselves.

As they talked, they kept their arms around each other's shoulders. Katie listened as they arranged for Jake to come back at the end of the day and get a massage. She watched as her boss stretched her neck, rolling her head to the side in an attempt to alleviate the tension that so often resided there.

Katie knew that, in spite of the fact that Elizabeth was a massage therapist and knew the need for them, she very rarely actually got massages herself. As she rotated her head though, Jake frowned and automatically began rubbing at the area. *Yeah,* Katie thought sarcastically, *no chance in hell.* She shook her head silently and watched as the pair continued their conversation, agreeing that Jake could come back in a few hours and Elizabeth would see him.

Watching the two of them, the casual observer would have thought they actually were together. She had. She still remembered the day she mentioned it to Elizabeth, asking how long they had been together. Her boss's face had flushed brightly and she had stammered a denial.

Another time, Nick had mentioned it to Jake at a family dinner and he had vehemently stated that there was "No way in hell." Katie knew that all three of the men considered Elizabeth to be a part of their family, but the way Jake looked at her was not the way a man looked at his sister. She had never mentioned it again but that didn't stop her from thinking it every time she saw them together. She hid a small smile now as they continued to talk and finalized the time for Jake to come back later.

Jake and his brothers were the only male clients Elizabeth would take while she was alone. It wasn't that she was necessarily scared, she just knew that a lot of times, people still held in their minds the other connotation of massage.

Most people still didn't see it as a therapy but rather a luxury and in the case of some men, a sinful pleasure to be completed in a most inappropriate fashion.

Fortunately, Elizabeth had only had a couple of clients who stepped out of line and they had only done so once. Still, it was her policy for her protection and theirs that someone else had to be in the office if she was seeing a male client. She knew Jake and his brothers would never cause problems so she'd never thought twice about making an exception for them.

As they talked, Elizabeth's client reappeared from the back, looking refreshed and relaxed. This was what Elizabeth loved about her job. There was nothing like it in the world.

Clients would come in stiff and sore, not moving the way they should be able to. She could see the pain or discomfort in their eyes, in their movements, just the way they carried themselves. Then, a short hour or so later, they would emerge a totally different person.

It was an obvious difference usually, they were smiling and happy and able to move freely again. For Elizabeth, to know that she had been able to make that difference, was an amazing thing. To see that for one person, for that one day, she had been able to improve their day, their life, it was an absolutely incredible feeling. That was what made every second of every single thing she had gone through to get where she was, worth it.

Some clients would tip her, which was always nice. Others would just thank her and be on her way. A few rare ones would go out of their way to tell her just how much she had helped them. Even if they said nothing though, she still had that knowledge inside that she had made a difference.

There was no way she could ever make a difference for people the way Jake did. She could never do his job, but she was still able to help in smaller ways. For her, that was enough.

Three clients later, Katie poked her head into one of the two massage rooms the small practice housed. Elizabeth was changing out the linens from the last client of the day in preparation for Jake's arrival. She had just started stripping the table when Katie came to say goodnight.

Elizabeth smiled at the younger woman and paused in her chore to talk for a moment. Katie told her she had closed everything up in the front and shut down the computers. She would see her in the morning.

They heard the bell over the front door and Katie turned to see Jake making his way through the lobby and down the hallway. Katie was quite a bit shorter than Elizabeth and Jake towered over her as he approached. He was a good looking man, even she could see that. And she knew damn well Elizabeth knew it too.

If it was just his raw appeal, Katie wouldn't have been so adamant. But they were both so smart, and shared the same sense of humor. They were two of the kindest people she knew and had known them both long enough to know that you didn't mess with one unless you wanted to deal with the other. They always had each other's back.

Katie waved and said one final good night to Elizabeth before repeating the same to Jake and making her way down the hall. She hurried out to the lobby once more to grab her purse and keys. Seconds later, she was out the front door, locking it behind her to prevent anyone else entering the establishment.

Back in the massage room, Jake leaned easily against the door casing and watched Elizabeth. It never ceased to amaze him how quickly she could strip the table and have it remade with almost military precision. Three quick moves and the sheets and face cradle cover were gone.

Seconds later, a new cover was in place and she was spreading the first of two sheets on the table. A top sheet joined it, followed quickly by a blanket. There was no wasted motion and she moved quickly and silently as she performed the task. The entire process took less than two minutes and looked as if it had taken far longer.

She finished by folding down one side of the blanket and top sheet, then smoothed the blanket and was done. Jake reached down for the used items that had been discarded on the floor and handed them to Elizabeth. He knew she washed all the laundry herself and would go drop them in the laundry while he undressed and got on the table.

As he prepared for the session, he looked around the room. Much like the lobby and Elizabeth's own apartment, the decor was simple and understated. The colors in this room were different from the ones in the lobby. This room was a silver color on three walls and a light purple on the fourth. There was little furniture in the room, the massage table taking up the majority of floor space in the small area. Aside from that was a stool, on which Elizabeth sat for some portions of her sessions, and a small stand in the corner.

The top of the stand held a small digital clock, not exactly cohesive with the style of the rest of the room, but necessary for time-keeping purposes. It also boasted a small battery-operated candle for atmosphere and one of those speaker stations for MP3 players. That was where the music came from. All in all, Elizabeth had done an amazing job of maximizing the space and creating a place that tricked one into relaxing before they even realized they'd done so.

A light tap at the door announced Elizabeth's return and preceded her entry into the room. Despite the fact that he was not a regular client, she always insisted on the same lighting and music that she used for everyone else. Even though they had their normal conversations, she always maintained the professional boundaries required of her station.

Face down, he was unable to see her but he could smell her warm, sweet scent. He could also hear the whisper of her clothes as she moved around the table, adjusting the blankets, slipping the bolster under his ankles and then fussing with the face cradle. Finally, she asked softly if everything was comfortable. Just like she always did.

After his approval, he felt the gentle but firm pressure of her hands on each shoulder blade through the covers. She would press lightly for a moment before stretching his back, he knew.

Then she would fold the blanket down to the top of his hips before bringing the sheet down to the same level. After that she would carefully tuck the sheet under each hip to secure it.

The first touch of her hands on his bare skin always made him jump. It wasn't that it startled him. It was just something about *her* hands on his skin that sent a jolt through his body.

He lay quietly as the steady rhythmic stroking began. Firmly, her palms glided from his shoulders, down either side of his spine, stopping just at the top of his hips before making a U-turn and retreating to his shoulders. Her fingers slid around the sides of his shoulders, curving down to the front, then back up the side of his neck to the base of his skull.

Her movements were smooth and measured. Each stroke calculated but easy. The usual relaxing warmth began to spread through him as she worked her magic. They talked as she massaged his back, gradually working deeper into the tense muscles that were always tighter than she would like.

Elizabeth kneaded the taut tissue of his shoulders, shaking her head slightly as she asked him for the hundredth time if he was following the suggestions she'd given him. Stretching, heating pad, water, and more frequent massage were all things she'd nagged him about for years. She knew he at least tried on some of them, but he would never come more than once a month for his massages. He told her it wasn't right. Because she wouldn't accept payment from him, he was not coming any more frequently than that.

He'd been worked on enough now though, that he could usually tell which part of her arm or hand she was using. Sometimes, she would use knuckles. Other times would be thumbs or forearms. Because it was so intense, she would only rarely use her elbows. Still, sometimes it was necessary and he never minded. The relief it brought was worth any temporary discomfort.

As he was thinking this, he smiled faintly. She was using her palms again. Sometimes when she did that, he would get this strange feeling he couldn't quite describe. It was happening now though. He'd never told her about it for fear she'd think he was crazy, but sometimes when she was running her palms or fingertips over his skin, it would feel like a mild electric current was flowing from her body to his. It wasn't enough to be uncomfortable, just strange and he didn't want to risk offending her or making her think he was nuts.

He remembered helping her study when she

was in massage school and vaguely recalled something about Chi. Chi was the life force that flowed through every living being and he remembered something about a modality that used that energy for healing purposes. Perhaps that was it. Either way, he sure as hell wasn't saying anything.

Gradually, Elizabeth sank her fingers deeper into the muscles she was working on and his thoughts refocused on her movements. Jake was always tight, as were most of her clients, in the upper back and shoulders. That was pretty much a normal thing, but some were worse than others. Considering his line of work and the incredible amount of physical and emotional stress he put himself through daily, it was unsurprising that Jake was one of the worst.

The silver lining of that was that Jake never complained when she went a little deeper than she probably should. He could take the pressure she felt he needed to work out the kinks and knots that seemed to be as much a part of him as his arms or legs. Ignoring his body, not becoming distracted by the fact that she was touching Jake this way, was the only issue she had. Jake was the only man who caused that complication, too.

It wasn't anything she ever acted on or even

mentioned to him. She viewed it more as a guilty pleasure than anything else. In the confines of the treatment room, she was free to touch him as much as she wanted. It would never be anything unprofessional. She was far too disciplined for that. But nothing said she couldn't enjoy the pleasure of touching a gorgeous man's body.

Conversation became slightly more difficult for Jake as she lay her forearm across one side of his lower back and pressed down a little. There was more pressure and the lower part of her arm slid up the powerful muscles that flanked his spine. She followed the cord of muscle all the way up between his shoulder blade and the vertebrae of his upper back.

The strength of her small hands always amazed him. It didn't seem possible that they could be strong enough to do the job they did day after day. Her hands were capable of eliciting a strange blend of pain and soothing. He had no idea how it worked, just that it did.

Elizabeth was able to take him just to the edge of too much pain but never quite over. A combination of forearms, knuckles, and elbows ensured that her hands didn't get overused. For a woman with her build - not overly muscular - she was deceptively strong, able to exert a shocking amount of pressure.

A small smile graced his lips as he thought of the many times he'd heard and seen men come into Elizabeth's office, thinking they were tough and that just because she was female, she "couldn't hurt" them. They were usually proven wrong within moments and he could not help being more than a little amused every time. He suspected that it secretly amused and pleased her as well, not that she'd ever admit to it.

Elizabeth eased off the pressure a little as she finished up his back. She always spent a little longer on his back than anywhere else. Legs would get a few minutes, he knew. Then, she would turn him over and he could watch her.

He loved watching her as she worked. Her face was a unique blend of studied concentration and complete relaxation. This was truly her element. Hers were hands that were meant to heal and they did, often.

Even draping and undraping, her movements were smooth and easy. She would lift the limb in question, move the sheet as needed and gently replace it, taking no more than a second or two and hardly disturbing the client. Then, just as seamlessly she would resume her massage. Sometimes he would catch her with her eyes closed, lost in a world he would never enter.

He'd asked her about it once. She had been

working on him and he had looked up to see her, still working but her eyes shut to the world. He had asked if she was okay.

Her eyes had opened instantly. They were clear and alert, not tired like he'd expected. He knew she worked a lot and wondered honestly if she was tired.

"Of course, I'm fine," she'd replied, "Why?"

"Just wondering. Your eyes were closed."

"Oh," she had murmured softly. "I, um, I do that sometimes."

"Why?"

He had been unable to help the curiosity that drove the question.

She had paused, uncertain how to explain to him the reason for it. Some people thought it was strange, or that she was strange. He wouldn't, but it was still difficult to explain to someone who hadn't experienced it.

"I can see better sometimes," she began. "Closing my eyes lets me concentrate more on what I'm doing. Fewer distractions."

She had continued her smooth, even rhythm while she spoke.

"I listen to my fingers. They tell me a lot. I can feel things in the muscles I'm touching. If I listen to my hands, it tells me what I need to know. I can tell a lot just by paying attention to what they tell me."

He'd nodded and watched her for a moment, sensing she was trying to decide whether to end her explanation there or continue. His continued silence encouraged her and she hesitantly elaborated a bit more. Sometimes, she'd expounded a little, she could "see" the muscles under the skin. She could sense the trouble areas without them actually being visible to the average eye.

Once more, he'd nodded, considering her response. He wasn't quite sure what to say. It was certainly an interesting concept and she apparently believed that it helped her. Whether it did or not, she gave one hell of a massage. So, he certainly was not going to argue the point.

Now, he opened his eyes as she finally moved to the head of the table. His favorite part was this. When she had turned him over and finished everything else, she would work on his neck and shoulders, occasionally doing a little bit of light work on his face and scalp. Her face was sometimes mere inches from his. And if he tried, he could catch a faint hint of her familiar scent. Occasionally, he could feel her warmth as she moved over him.

She closed the session after stretching his neck a bit, and he opened his eyes once more. The lights were still dim but he could see her face, relaxed and peaceful as it always was at the end of their sessions. He wondered if it was always that way. He knew that sometimes the sessions would drain her because she would be exhausted at the end of the day.

Earlier, she had looked like she had been that tired again, but now she seemed almost slightly renewed. He knew it was silly but kind of hoped it was the easy conversation and company of a friend that had provided her with a second wind of sorts.

"I'll be back in a minute ok?" she announced and turned to leave.

"Ok, thanks."

As always, he had to fight through the "post massage coma" as he called it, the languorous feeling that lingered following the massage. The relaxed effect slowed his redressing and left him really wanting a nap. At the same time, he felt oddly refreshed. Now, it was time to take his friend out for dinner and maybe a movie…or…he grinned as he got an even better idea.

# Chapter 4

An hour or so later, the pair sat in the cool night air, cheering on the local minor league baseball team. Elizabeth had always loved baseball and Jake loved watching her watch it. Her face was so alive and animated. She screamed and cheered and swore at the umpires as much as any man he knew.

Close games would have her on the edge of her seat and he would watch as she all but held her breath. Not many women he knew were into the sport like she was. Hell, most of the women he knew probably didn't even know what baseball even was. Without a doubt though, none of them would be as much fun here as she was.

The top of the ninth inning came and Elizabeth was on her feet. Clapping and yelling encouragement, he smiled widely as he watched her. The home team got their third out and she squealed with delight and hugged him. Her excitement was contagious and he found himself getting caught up in the moment.

She was chewing her lip again, waiting and

hoping the home team would get the run that would seal their victory. The first batter struck out and she groaned. The next hitter got on base and she seemed to be even more anxious. Jake half expected to see her fall over, she was leaning so far forward.

The tied game bottom of the ninth, two outs, full count excitement was apparently not a myth, he decided. He couldn't tell, though, if it was his own enthusiasm that was getting him so on edge, or if it was carryover from the woman at his side. The last hitter came to the plate and Elizabeth was chanting, "Come on, come on, come on" under her breath. Jake felt her small hand in his own and wondered if she even knew she had grabbed it.

The pitcher threw the ball and the bat cracked. Everyone watched as the ball sailed through the air. It passed the infield, continued through the air in the outfield and he chuckled as Elizabeth squeezed his hand tighter.

It cleared the fence and the crowd roared. Elizabeth screamed and jumped up and down, hugging him and they shared a celebratory kiss. Suddenly, they both seemed to realize what they were doing and froze. Their eyes locked for a moment before Elizabeth backed away, breaking the trance they seemed to have been caught up in.

Jake felt a sense of loss as she withdrew and tried to shake it off. That was just the sort of thought he didn't need, he told himself. He should really call Allison.

Allison was the gorgeous blond he had been seeing casually for a few months. She was everything most guys would want. Even though his attachment to her was purely physical, he hoped it would get his mind off of Elizabeth and back where it should be.

Elizabeth had been seeing someone too, he knew. Perhaps it was time he met the man. They could have a double date, he thought. Maybe the combination of being with Allison and seeing Elizabeth with another man would finally do the trick to get her out of his system and off his mind.

A few moments later, they were caught in the crush of the crowd leaving the stadium. It was surprising actually, how many fans had shown up to a minor league game. The ebb and flow of people around them kept bumping Elizabeth and Jake together. While Elizabeth seemed unphased, Jake was slowly losing his mind.

Every few steps, she would be jostled against him and he could feel the softly curved breasts against his arm, or her hip against his. Trying to protect what little sanity he had left, he suggested that she walk in front of him so that he could keep people from pushing her out of the way. At least, that was what he told her.

Much to his dismay, he found that his idea only made matters worse. Instead of being shoved together side to side, he was pressed into intimate contact with her backside. Though the contact was more fleeting, it was no less maddening and he could feel their bodies touching from shoulder to hip.

At last, they were clear of the turnstiles and made their way through the rapidly dispersing crowd to Jake's truck. Tonight had been fun, he admitted, but perhaps too much fun. He was reminded once more of his notion to set up a double date night and mentioned it to Elizabeth now.

For some unknown reason, her reaction was less than thrilled. Perhaps, she preferred the one on one time with her man, and saw the idea of a foursome as interrupting her plans. Jake hesitated for a moment, wondering if it was such a good idea to pursue his plan in that case. The whole point had been to spend time with Allison to get his mind off of Elizabeth. At the same time, he'd been hoping that seeing Elizabeth with her boyfriend would help him remember that she was out of bounds where he was concerned. Now, however, he was wondering if that was going to work out the way he'd hoped.

Given the unreasonable spark of jealousy that shot through him at the thought of Elizabeth kissing another man the way she'd kissed him moments before, he doubted it. He had to try though. This was driving him insane. He needed something to help him regain perspective and if watching Elizabeth and her man together didn't do it, nothing would.

That Friday night, Elizabeth and Jake met up and headed to one of the local restaurants for their double date. This would also serve as the perfect opportunity for him to play big brother and warn her date against hurting her. As long as Elizabeth didn't find out, he'd be ok. Of course, if she did, he was dead.

They walked into the restaurant together and Jake immediately spotted Allison in a corner booth. She was, as always, dressed to kill. Every hair was in place, her make-up perfectly applied. Still, somehow, he was having trouble forgetting about the woman at his side and focusing his attention on his date. Even though they were nowhere near being serious, the gorgeous blond should have captured his full mind. Instead, all he could think of was the redhead walking beside him.

Jake had picked Elizabeth up about half an hour before. When he'd seen her standing there, it had taken every ounce of self-control to battle down the twin urges to take her in his arms and kiss her till she forgot every man but him, or to tell her to go back in and put some more clothes on. She looked stunning.

The thought occurred to him that, in different circumstances, this could have been their own date, not a double with another couple. He pushed away the thought along with the question of why he wished so badly the other two members of the party were not going to be there. Wasn't that the whole reason he'd conjured up this idea? To remind himself that they were both with other people and that Elizabeth was off limits. That was a fact that, to his dismay, he seemed to be forgetting more and more often lately.

He looked down at her now as she walked beside him. The simple green dress she wore made her eyes glow and set off the highlights in her hair. Several male heads turned their way as they entered the establishment and Jake unconsciously tucked her a little closer to his side. In an unmistakable challenge to any man in the room, he glanced around as he pulled her body nearer to his. Even as he did so, he was completely oblivious to the equal amount of female attention he was drawing as they moved through the dark and crowed room.

Part of the building was a bar and club, the other part a restaurant. The part they were in was the bar area and very dimly lit. Louder than necessary music filled the air, making conversation difficult. That didn't seem to be a major issue though, as most of the occupants seemed to be otherwise engaged and conversation was not a huge concern.

Elizabeth looked nervous as she searched the room for her date. He wasn't with Allison and Jake wondered where the man was. He hoped she didn't get stood up. A glance at Elizabeth revealed exactly what he thought he would see, her lower lip once again caught between her teeth, tugging at it.

"He'll be here." Jake assured her with a gentle squeeze.

Elizabeth couldn't help the nervous habit of gnawing on her lip even as Jake's arm warm across the bare skin of her back comforted her. She swallowed a comment as his date, Allison, spotted them and poutily made her way over to them. He didn't miss the baleful look tossed to Elizabeth as she came up and wrapped herself around him. She planted a lusty kiss dead on his mouth, one that he knew was designed to warn Elizabeth away and stake her claim on him.

An amused grin tugged at Elizabeth's lips as she watched Allison's possessive behavior and she tried not to laugh out loud. Even after being told repeatedly that Elizabeth was just a best friend, like a sister, Allison still didn't trust her. Or maybe it was Jake she didn't trust. Who knew?

In the last two weeks, he'd seen her with no less than three different men. He hadn't bothered saying anything because he honestly didn't care. He enjoyed spending time with her and enjoyed the occasional nights together, but that was it. It was beyond him why she was so possessive and jealous.

Elizabeth looked around the restaurant again for Mark. She'd only been out with the man a few times, and those only to placate Lexi, who had played matchmaker. In all honesty, she hadn't really liked him.

Something about him just set her teeth on edge and she felt almost actually uncomfortable around him. She had managed thus far to make sure they weren't alone together anywhere. She'd only met him in public places and always drove herself.

The trio headed back to the corner table Allison had been occupying when they had arrived and sat down. Elizabeth looked around the room surreptitiously, wondering where Mark was. He was late, again. He had been for all three of their other dates too.

Truth be told, she wasn't too upset about it. Mark was nothing more than a distraction from her obsession with Jake at best, and at worst an annoyance she was seriously considering getting rid of. She wouldn't be entirely devastated if he just didn't show up.

Jake's hand on her arm brought her back to their cozy little table and she met his eyes. He had apparently said something, but she hadn't even heard him. Apologetically, she asked him to repeat it.

A tight look came to his face as he surveyed her own pinched features. She knew he was misinterpreting her expression as worry that her date might not show. That was okay with her though. Better to let him think that she was worried about that than that she didn't actually want him to come at all.

"I asked what you wanted to drink," he answered softly. "Amaretto sour?"

She nodded, not speaking, and toyed with the napkin in front of her. Her cell phone buzzed and she looked at it and rolled her eyes. Mark had texted her that he was late again and would be there shortly. She sighed. Of course. So, now she was stuck with Jake, whom she couldn't get out of her mind anyway, and his little lovey-dovey Barbie doll girlfriend who was getting more annoying by the second.

Now she was clinging to Jake and sulking because Jake was asking Elizabeth about her text. He shot the other woman a warning look, which she ignored and pouted prettily at him, trying to coax him closer for another territory marking kiss. Instead he gently but firmly removed her hands from his arm and spoke quietly in her ear.

Elizabeth couldn't hear what was being said but whatever it was, Allison was not pleased. She shot Elizabeth a poisonous look and picked up her drink, draining half of it in one go. Elizabeth couldn't help a small satisfied smirk as Jake turned his attention to her once more.

With a wicked glint in her eyes, she leaned over and covered his hand with hers. She intentionally injected a rather intimate tone in her voice as she explained the text she'd received.

"I'm afraid it will be a while, dear," she murmured throatily, placing a slight emphasis on the endearment.

She pretended not to notice the increasing fury of Jake's companion as she explained that he said that he would be there as soon as he could. Something in her couldn't resist making it seem as though she had planned the whole thing. Looking deeply into his eyes, she kissed his cheek lingering just a fraction of a second too long. To add to it, she laid her hand lovingly on his other cheek for a moment before pulling away and raising an eyebrow at the sultry vixen on the other side of him. The older woman was glaring daggers at her and Elizabeth raised a brow in silent challenge.

She sat back against the seat and a glimmer of laughter appeared deep in Jake's eyes, telling Elizabeth he was on to her little game. Elizabeth had never been possessive of him. But, on occasion, when the girl of the moment was being so, it amused her to pull out all the stops and put on the show of being his favorite girl. She never went too far with it, just enough to remind the other woman that she had been there first and wasn't going anywhere.

A tall blond man made his way through the crowd to their table and slid in beside Elizabeth and she greeted him coolly, accepting the kiss he intended for her mouth on her cheek instead. He looked slightly chastened though still full enough of himself that Jake itched to wipe the smug look off of his face. Especially when he realized that Mark was one of the men he'd seen Allison with earlier that week.

He glanced at Allison now, watching her expression which was fully trained on the newest member of their party. With an inward sigh, he resigned himself to breaking things off with her after Elizabeth had gone. He didn't want her to be hurt by knowing what was going on.

There wasn't much point in pretending that he was actually upset about Allison's behavior. After all, hadn't he kissed Elizabeth more than once himself? At any rate, it was no more and no less than he expected from her. The only thing that bothered him about it was the possibility of Elizabeth getting hurt. That, he would not allow. When he broke it off, he would make sure to tell Allison to stay away from Mark.

As for Mark, Jake had a few words in mind for him. Even though he told himself it was none of his business how serious the relationship between Elizabeth and the other man was, it took a lot of willpower to keep from planting his fist in the younger man's face. He tried again to kiss Elizabeth, who once more averted her face and it was Jake's turn to be amused.

The waitress came by with the drinks Elizabeth and Jake had ordered. She took Mark's order and Jake clenched his jaw at the way the other man flirted with the waitress right in front of Elizabeth. She either didn't notice or was pretending not to and judging by the fact that her drink was half gone already, he was guessing it was the latter. Her setting the empty glass on the table confirmed it and he almost stopped her as she cut across her date's flirting with the waitress to order another drink.

Allison also ordered another round and he almost wished she'd make it a double. She was much easier to deal with when she was drunk. At least, it was easier for *him* to deal with her that way. He knew that was bad, but it was true.

Mark asked Elizabeth to dance and they left the table, although Jake sensed it was rather reluctant on her part. As they walked away, he could hear Mark laying on the charm. He complimented Elizabeth on how gorgeous she looked and apologized for being late. Jake noticed that he put his arm around her with his hand resting squarely on her backside.

His eyes followed them around as they danced and Allison grew more impatient. Given what he knew, Jake was having a hard time pretending to feel guilty about it. It was tempting to end things now, so that he didn't have to pretend. But once more, for Elizabeth's sake, he was going to suck it up till later on. Once she and her date left, he would let the woman beside him know precisely where she stood. Till then, he supposed he should pretend to pay attention to her. Still his eyes occasionally wandered and he watched Elizabeth move Mark's hand from her derriere to her hip at least three times. She had also avoided several attempts to kiss her.

Elizabeth was growing tired of having to move Mark's hand off her backside and told him so. He smiled and murmured something about not being able to resist because she looked so hot. Her temper already frayed, Elizabeth told him bluntly that if she had to move his hand again, the evening was over. He gave a long-suffering sigh and dutifully moved his hand to her waist, inquiring petulantly if he was being punished because he'd been late.

"Mark, I don't think this is working out for us," she began as she moved his hand once more.

"I think it's working great, baby," he murmured moving in for another attempt at a kiss.

Elizabeth dodged the attempt by laying her head on his shoulder. She would like to say it was all him and the way he flirted with any woman around even when she was sitting right beside him. However, if she was completely honest, it had a lot more to do with the brown-eyed man whose gaze had barely left her since she and Mark headed toward the dance floor.

"No, Mark. It's not working out for me. I don't think I can do this. I just don't think it's...I don't know. It just doesn't feel right."

"Well if it's about feelings baby, I'll give you something to feel," he murmured suggestively.

A disgusted sigh left her mouth and she attempted to put a little distance between them.

"You have got to be kidding me," she said hopefully.

"You know I want you, baby."

"I don't know. I think you were more interested in the waitress than me. You were flirting with her while I was sitting right there," she added.

"I was just being friendly," he disagreed.

"No. There is being friendly and there's flirting and I may not be the smartest woman ever but even I can tell the difference between the two."

"Fine. I'm sorry," he attempted to mollify her.

"Now, can we kiss and make up?"

"No, Mark. This isn't a kiss and make up thing. It's not just you flirting with the waitress either. The feeling isn't there. I just don't think we are meant to be together."

"Sure we are. Look, I have a hotel room. When we get done here, what do you say we go and I'll show you how much you mean to me, ok?" he murmured in her ear.

"You're not getting this. You don't seem to understand. I do not want to be with you. I'm sorry. "

"Awww, come on baby. Give me one more chance, please?" he wheedled.

Elizabeth sighed and shook her head, laying it on his shoulder once more to avoid his umpteenth attempt to kiss her. She was grateful when the song ended at last and she was able to escape. It was all she could do to not run off the floor and away from him.

"I need to use the little girls' room," she said as they crossed the room toward the table where Jake and Allison sat waiting.

Pausing only long enough to grab the fresh drink that had been left for her during the dance, Elizabeth drained the contents in one go. Softly, she repeated her excuse to the remaining occupants of the table and requested that should the waitress return, could someone please order her another drink.

Leaving the table, Elizabeth could feel Jake's eyes on her as she made her escape. His companion was also watching, though her eyes were boring holes through her. She couldn't have cared less at the moment though. She was so completely over this date.

She was over Mark and his flirting. Allison and her jealousy were no better. She was even getting irritated with Jake although she had no clue why. Perhaps she should leave soon.

Her hand pushed the door to the ladies' room open and she leaned against it with a sigh. Eyes closed, she rested there for a moment before making her way to the sinks that lined one wall. Maybe a splash of cold water would help revive her a little. She could hope, right?

It didn't make any sense to her honestly. Why did Mark's flirting irritate her so when she was certainly no better? Jake had kissed her and she hadn't been able to stop thinking about it. She would rather be with Jake any time than Mark. Even when she'd been dancing with Mark, she'd been surreptitiously glancing at Jake and Allison. What was wrong with her? A lot, a sardonic voice in her head replied.

The door opened again and Allison entered the room, her eyes trained on Elizabeth. Her bright red lips pinched shut as she eyed the younger woman balefully. She raised her chin slightly as she walked into the room.

"You look tired, dear. Perhaps you should call it a night and head home with that gorgeous guy of yours," her tone was sweet, but Elizabeth easily detected the icy venom hidden in her words.

"I appreciate your concern," Elizabeth replied coolly. "I'm good. Jake and I came together and will leave together."

Her firm tone and words didn't sit well with Allison and her eyes narrowed. Elizabeth turned and leaned a hip against the sink as her eyes twinkled with amusement. The older woman was quite obviously looking for trouble. Elizabeth was more than happy to play along, for now.

"You know, after he drops you off, he's going to spend the night with me, right?"

"Yes," Elizabeth shrugged. "But you do know that after you're gone, I'll still be here right?"

"Honey, you're so delusional. Jake is a player. He will only keep you in his life as long as it suits him. You aren't his type so don't con yourself into believing he will ever love you back."

Elizabeth drew in a sharp breath, surprised at the impact of the woman's verbal blow. She saw the glint of victory in Allison's eyes. Even as she wanted to deny the implication, she wasn't completely sure she could. After all, hadn't he told her exactly the same thing all those years ago?

As if she were reading Elizabeth's mind, Allison pressed her advantage.

"Don't try to deny it. It's quite obvious to anyone with eyes. Jake really is so sweet to pretend ignorance. Or perhaps he truly is oblivious to your feelings. After all, we have been together for a while now. I have no doubt where his affections lie."

Elizabeth remained silent, telling herself to ignore the words she was hearing. She knew Jake far better than Allison did. That wasn't Jake at all. Still, Allison was right. Jake would never love her. He had told her that himself, hadn't he?

The earlier amusement and confidence was gone, replaced now with a dull ache deep in her chest. Determined to not show her pain, she pasted a smile on her face and leaned closer to the other woman so she could be heard with little more than a whisper. She kept her tone as saccharinely sweet as Allison's had been moments ago.

"You do know there's a difference between sex and affection, right? No, I suppose you wouldn't, would you?"

Allison looked slightly taken aback and Elizabeth pressed her advantage, "Even so, you may be right about where his affections lie, 'honey'," Elizabeth purred. "But, in love with me or not, I was here long before he knew your name, and I'll be by his side long after he's forgotten it again."

She straightened and strode to the door, casually looking over her shoulder before stepping through it, "By the way, you have something between your teeth."

Jake watched as Elizabeth headed toward the restrooms, with Mark hot on her heels. No doubt, she was trying to escape and he couldn't blame her. Mark was grating on his nerves and appeared to be doing the same to Elizabeth. Still, until he heard otherwise, he would play nice. He would refrain from rearranging the man's features until he was certain Elizabeth wouldn't do the same to him.

Allison had been watching the pair as well and suddenly decided that a trip to the facilities might not be such a bad idea. A faint smile appeared on Jake's lips as he imagined the conversation that would ensue. He had no worry for Elizabeth. She could handle herself. He almost pitied Allison though. Almost.

This was not a bad opportunity for him to talk to Elizabeth's date though. A few words of warning might be in order. He rose and walked over to where the younger man was lurking in the hallway outside the door to the room where the two women had disappeared.

Mark looked up as Jake approached. Apparently completely oblivious to the undertones of hostility in Jake's gaze, Mark smiled and leaned in closer to whisper his question.

"So, man, you know Elizabeth pretty well. Can you help a guy out? What does she like? How can I, you know, score?"

Jake remained silent for a moment, taken aback by the sheer audacity of the question. He reminded himself that Elizabeth would have his ass if he decked Mark like he wanted to. His eyes narrowed in warning though.

"No. Sorry, I can't."

"Well, I mean you know what she likes right? You've known her for a while. Have you, you know, had her? Is she good? What can a guy do to make points? She's shutting me down all over the place. How can I get some action?"

Jake's jaw clenched so tightly he was afraid he might crack a tooth.

"You can't. And I will tell you right now, if you hurt her, I will tear you apart with my bare hands. Do you understand?"

Mark looked vaguely worried for a moment, before he relaxed and laughed again.

"Ah, so you struck out. Well don't worry, I think I'm man enough to take up the challenge and beat it. So you can drop the best friend, big brother, protector act huh? I get it, buddy. I'll be very respectful," he said silkily.

Jake took one step closer, towering menacingly over the shorter guy as he glowered down at him. He kept his tone low and icy, barely more than a growl.

"It's no act, I assure you. You hurt her in any way, shape or form, and you will wish you had never been born. That is *not* a threat. It is a promise. Remember it."

With that, he stepped into the other door in the hallway, effectively cutting off any reply Mark may have had. Maybe a splash of cold water on his face would help cool him off. Otherwise, he might just do something he would regret.

Elizabeth emerged from the bathroom, her

head held high and almost groaned when she realized Mark was there waiting for her. He took her arm, intent on leading her back to the dance floor. Resigned, she allowed him to lead the way. She could tolerate one more dance then would plead sore feet for the remainder of the evening.

Seemingly attempting to make up for earlier, Mark kept his hands appropriately placed throughout most of the song. He only tried to kiss her three times. Then he mentioned the hotel room again. Elizabeth sighed again and laid her head on his shoulder once more, her face away from her partner, waiting for the song to end so she could escape again. Finally the last notes faded and she all but ran from the dance floor back toward the table.

Jake met them halfway, giving the smaller man a look intended to kill. There would definitely be words later, to say the least. Dismissing Mark, Jake turned his attention to Elizabeth.

"Mind if I claim a dance, lady?" he smiled, using the endearment he frequently bestowed on her. His face and tone were soft as he spoke to her.

She smiled gratefully, accepting the proffered hand and followed Jake onto the dance floor.

"You looked like you needed a break," he explained as they reached the edge of the crowded area set aside for dancing.

"Thanks. I did," she admitted gratefully.

Jake took her into his arms easily, pulling her close to him and Elizabeth's mouth went dry. Perhaps she hadn't thought this through too well after all. Jake had only held her like this a few times before. She wasn't prepared for the feel of his strong arms around her or the heat from his solid body radiating out and warming her own. Nor was she prepared for the suddenly weak feeling in her knees that had her leaning into him for support.

The sultry notes of the song seemed to thicken the air between them and Elizabeth swallowed hard. His body was every bit as hard and muscled as it had been eight years ago and she was close enough now to feel every bit of that body. She dared a tiny glance at him and found her gaze caught in his.

The song, something about slow dancing and flames, seemed to fit the moment because she was certain that somewhere nearby was a raging inferno. Even worse, it seemed to be getting dangerously closer as the song went on. The sexy beat thrummed through her body and she swayed perfectly in sync with his body as if they were meant to be just this way, fitting perfectly in his arms and against him.

Suddenly, she couldn't remember how to breathe and her heart hammered away at her ribs. She wondered if he could feel it. Forcing herself to look away, she chewed her lip again. Jake used one hand to gently release her lip and she met his heated look again. His hand remained cradling her cheek, the pad of his thumb tracing the curve of her lower lip.

God, he was killing her. She was so certain he was going to kiss her. But, she told herself adamantly, Jake was here with someone else and so was she. He would never…

But there was something different in his eyes as he looked at her now. Something hot and dangerous and oh so tempting. As if he were seeing her as a woman, not just his friend. It made her pulse flutter even more wildly as she remained transfixed, in his arms. Their bodies, in intimate contact, swayed to the music without any effort.

She could feel his breath on her face and neck, the teasing whisper setting her nerve endings ablaze. His hand on her bare lower back hadn't moved an inch but still was searing her skin. If possible, they moved even closer together, thigh to thigh and chest to chest, they moved.

It seemed to be getting unbearably hot for some reason, she realized. He'd done nothing though. Must be the drink, she thought. She had emptied it rather quickly. But she'd been drunk before and knew better. It was dancing that was doing it. Or, more specifically, dancing with this man was what was doing it.

She had never realized dancing could be such a turn on. Nor had she realized that being in such close proximity to Jake as she was now, would allow her to catch an occasional hint of the spicy woodsy scent he wore. Almost groaning aloud, she chose to avert her face by resting her head on his shoulder. As she did, she felt him stiffen.

"I'm sorry," she said lifting her head. "I just –"

She broke off when she realized his attention was not on her but on their table. Turning her head slightly, she saw why. Allison and Mark were all but making out together. She sighed and turned back to Jake, who was watching her face carefully.

"Oh, God, I'm sorry. I didn't know he would – "

Jake interrupted her gently.

"I'm not worried about her. Or him for that matter. I knew she was seeing other guys and had actually decided to break it off with her after leaving here tonight. I was more worried about you. I know that has to hurt, seeing him like that with someone else,"

She gave a bitter laugh.

"Not really. I'm not surprised. We've only seen each other a couple times and besides I'm not the type of-" she stopped, blinking hard then looked away again.

"The type of what?" he prompted, when she didn't continue.

"Nothing. Um, listen, I'm not feeling so well suddenly. I think I'm going to catch a cab and go home, okay? You stay here and enjoy the rest of the evening and I'll see you in the morning."

She kissed his cheek before turning out of his arms and heading toward the table determinedly. He followed, not sure what else to do, but knowing she was not leaving here alone. There was, after all, no reason for him to stay either.

As they approached the table, Allison and Mark jumped apart guiltily. Jake stood back for a moment, watching as Elizabeth pasted a friendly smile on her face and greeted them both as if nothing were wrong. She reached for her purse, careful not to touch either of the other two occupants.

"I'm not feeling well. I'm going home. Enjoy

the rest of the evening," she stated.

"I'll take you home," Mark offered smoothly.

"No," she refused, almost too fast. "That's ok. I'm just going to catch a cab."

"Well I'll call you then," he said.

"No, that's okay. You don't have to. In fact, I rather prefer you didn't. I can see you've found someone- I mean something- more interesting to do."

She kept her tone sweet as she reached for the fresh drink left for her, raised it in a mock toast and drained all but a few drops of it. Jake choked on his laughter when she just as sweetly reached over and poured the remainder of the contents over Mark's head and walked away.

Allison started to rise, but Jake stopped her.

"I'm taking Elizabeth home. You don't need to call me" he said calmly.

"But I-"

"As Elizabeth put it, I see you have found someone more interesting to do. Good night."

Without another word, he turned on his heel and took off after Elizabeth. That last bit of booze was going to hit her soon and he'd be damned if he was going to let her out of his sight like that. Especially as upset as she undoubtedly was.

He'd only taken a handful of steps when he

heard Mark's voice above the din. The other man had left the booth and was coming toward him, calling his name. He paused for a moment and Mark approached him.

"Don't worry about it. I can take her home. I'm her date so I'm the one she should be leaving with. Unless, of course," he paused then a nasty smile spread across his face. "You want her for yourself. Now, it makes sense. Well whatever man, enjoy the who-"

Mark never even saw it coming. Before he finished his sentence, Jake's right fist connected squarely with his jaw, knocking him flat on his back. He lay there for a moment, dazedly staring up at the man who had put him there.

There was a promise in Jake's eyes of far more than a simple right hook, if he dared to get up. Wisely, he stayed where he was, almost oblivious to Allison's arrival and subsequent fussing over him. His gaze was trained solely on the tall man who seemed to almost be daring him to get up.

"Never speak her name again. Never call her. And most of all, don't you ever speak of her that way again."

Then he walked away, leaving the pair staring dumbfounded after him. He hoped Elizabeth hadn't already left. That idiot had delayed him just long enough that it was possible for her to have taken off walking as he knew she would. Still, he had finally gotten to punch that jerk in the mouth as he'd wanted all evening, so it wasn't all bad.

Just outside the door, he found her, already removing her heels. She had one in her hand and was leaning against the wall of the club removing the other one. The shoe was being stubborn but finally released her foot and she stood, rather unsteadily and looked around for a second. She had just started walking when Jake grabbed her elbow to guide her to his truck.

"What are you doing? I thought you were staying here," she protested tipsily.

"I can stay here with a floozy who's been sleeping with four men this past week, and her latest conquest. Or I can take my best friend, who is drunk and hurting, back to her home and ensure she gets there safely. Let me think about that," he responded, his tone deceptively light.

"But-"

"Elizabeth?" he interrupted.

"Yeah?" she replied, stumbling against him.

"Get in the truck."

She started to argue but there was something in his expression that changed her mind and she meekly did as he said. She tried to at least. Her impaired state made it somewhat difficult and Jake found it necessary to assist her before closing the door and going around to the driver's side of the vehicle.

Closing the door, he sighed into the dim interior, looking over at the woman who had been the one constant in his life for the last ten years. No matter what had happened, she had been there for him. He'd tried to be there for her as much as he could but he knew he hadn't always done a good job.

Elizabeth sat with her head leaned back against the seat as her head started spinning crazily. She could feel Jake's eyes on her and made an effort to sit up straighter. It didn't work very well. Giving up, she settled for opening her eyes and looking back at him.

"What's wrong?" she asked, still slurring slightly.

His hand reached toward her and tenderly tucked a stray hair behind her ear. Oh hell, she realized, he felt sorry for her now. Because of what Mark had done, he was feeling bad for her.

"Look," she began unsteadily. "I'm okay about Mark. I just was upset he chose your girlfriend to… to…"

She paused, unable to find the words she was looking for. God, but she was dizzy. And way too hot. She had to get out of this dress. She reached for the strap and started to pull it down and an almost panicked Jake stopped her.

"What are you doing?" he growled, more harshly than he'd intended.

"It's too hot," she replied groggily.

"Well, wait till you get home," he said, turning up the air conditioning.

The last thing he needed was a naked Elizabeth in the seat beside him. Even a half naked Elizabeth was more than he could handle at the moment. He knew his resistance was already lowered from the way he'd reacted to her nearness as they'd danced.

She nodded and leaned back against the seat once more and was silent. She really had had no idea that people could be so cruel and heartless, she thought. It wasn't that she cared much for Mark yet, but the notion that some people could care so little about other people's feelings was what was bothering her.

Better now than six months from now, she pointed out to herself. At least she hadn't fallen for him yet. It was just that sometime, it would be nice to find a man who wanted her, only her, just as she was. Unaware that a single tear had escaped and was rolling down her cheek, she was surprised to feel Jake's finger brush it away as he drove.

With a sigh, he reached over and took her hand, intertwining his fingers through hers. They rode in silence for the remainder of the drive, each lost in their own thoughts. Elizabeth's thoughts at least, were swirling madly through her head. Lost in the haze of the alcohol she'd dumped down her throat, they made no sense.

She was thinking things she shouldn't be thinking. Jake's mouth on hers, his hands on her body, was one such thought. Jake buried deep inside her body, moving in and out of her, both of them writhing in pleasure on her big, otherwise empty bed, was another. Horrified, she turned away and looked out the window, trying to force the haziness away. The more she tried though, the more she found her thoughts muddling.

Her Jake was there with her though so she was safe. She knew that. Jake would never let anything happen to her. Jake had always protected her and been there for her. He was the best friend a girl could ever have and she loved him so much.

Jake's jaw tightened as the words left her lips. He tried to remind himself that she was drunk and had no idea what she was saying. He told himself that it was the alcohol talking, not her. She probably hadn't even realized she'd spoken out loud. Still, his heart beat a little faster and kept up the pace as he guided the truck through the darkened streets.

Elizabeth looked down at her lap, where her hand lay, still clasped in Jake's much bigger one. Not fully aware of what she was doing, she brought their joined hands to her lips and pressed a kiss to his knuckles before turning to stare sightlessly out the window again. They would be home soon, she knew and she didn't want to be alone. She was so tired of being alone. Jake wouldn't stay with her she knew, because it wouldn't "be right."

He jumped when she spoke suddenly, "Let's get something to eat."

The man looked at her as if she'd sprouted another head and then shook his.

"You need to get home," he said firmly.

"Don't wanna go home," she protested, her tone petulant.

"Yes you do, so you can lie down in your nice comfy bed," he said coaxingly.

"My big, empty bed," she muttered, barely louder than a whisper.

Red flags shot up all over Jake's consciousness at her words, knowing he was veering into dangerous territory. Granted it was someplace he'd been before, but he'd done his damnedest not to ever go back there. He'd been determined to never take advantage of her like that again.

"You'll be asleep soon enough and you won't even notice it," he murmured, not even sounding convincing to his own ears.

Elizabeth just sighed and continued to stare out her window.

Moments later, Jake pulled the truck into a parking space in front of her building. He sat there for a moment and Elizabeth cracked open an eye to look at him. Her head was spinning faster than before and that was all she dared to do.

She was just about to ask him what was wrong when he moved and opened the door to climb out and come around to help her out of the truck. The door opened and as carefully as she could, Elizabeth turned to face Jake and tried to climb out. The end result was her all but falling onto him and him catching her against him. His arms wrapped around her tight, holding her up so she wouldn't fall.

Jake gritted his teeth as he helped Elizabeth up to her apartment. In her inebriated state, she stumbled against him several times, her soft curves jostling against his hard, lean frame. He barely withheld a sigh of relief when they finally made it to her apartment door.

Taking her keys from her hand, he made quick work of the lock and led Elizabeth inside. He closed the door behind them, still not relinquishing his hold on her. Gently, he sat her in a chair and removed the heels she had put back on in the truck.

She looked tired, he realized and was not in the least surprised. He slipped off his own shoes quickly as he took hers to the closet to put them away for her. When he returned, he found Elizabeth had abandoned the chair and was staring blankly out the window into the darkness.

Jake had no clue what else to do so he crossed the room till he stood behind her. His arms went around her and she relaxed back against his chest. Her chest rose and fell in a sigh as her fingers lightly stroked the arms that held her. Without thinking, she lifted one lean callused hand to her mouth and pressed her lips to it gently, much as she had done moments ago in the truck.

Between that simple gesture and the warmth of her lush feminine body so close to his own, Jake was certain the whole apartment had gone up in flames. Still, she needed him now. She needed her friend and he was going to be there. They stood like that for what seemed like hours, though in reality was only a few minutes.

"You okay?" he murmured after a while, knowing the question was stupid even as it left his lips.

*Idiot*, he chided himself. She was heartbroken. Of course she wasn't okay.

She nodded wordlessly, but her body shuddered with the effort of controlling her emotions. He tightened his arms around her slightly and shook his head. That was Elizabeth. She would never admit her heart was broken. He knew that.

"You don't have to pretend with me," he whispered. "In fact, I rather prefer you didn't."

Elizabeth sighed and leaned into him once more. God, if only it could always be like this. This was how it should be. Why couldn't he see that?

Now, he seemed to be waiting for her to say something. She sighed and shook her head. How could she explain to him that she truly wasn't devastated about the events of the evening? This was what she wanted. Right here. She just wanted to be here with Jake, just like this.

Was that so wrong? Surely, they could be happy together if he'd just give her a chance. But he wouldn't. She knew that. He'd made that crystal clear. Once more, the pain from his words that night shot through her being and she flinched.

Jake felt Elizabeth's sudden movement and wondered what had caused it. He hadn't moved so he knew he hadn't done anything. Then she sighed and relaxed against him again. Maybe it had been his imagination. For now, he just would enjoy holding her.

After a while though, Jake's curiosity got the better of him and he asked her the question that had been plaguing his mind since before they had left the restaurant.

"When we were dancing and you saw Allison and Mark, you started to say something," he began and felt her stiffen slightly against him.

She waited silently, waiting for him to continue even though she knew what was coming. It was really not information that she wanted to volunteer since she knew that he would take exception to the comment. Still, it was the way things seemed to her.

"You said something about not being the type of girl for something. What did you mean?" he finished when she didn't speak.

Elizabeth chewed her lip and debated pretending she hadn't heard his inquiry. She knew better though. He could see right through her and it would only confirm for him that she was upset.

She shrugged slightly before stepping out of the warm comfort that was Jake. For some reason, she felt the need to take a few steps away before answering him. Finally she smiled, somewhat bitterly, before she replied.

"I'm not the kind of girl that guys want to stay with, Jake. I'm not the kind of girl guys want."

Jake opened his mouth to speak but Elizabeth shook her head.

"Don't. Please," she entreated. "Please spare me your pity and don't patronize me. I know it. I have for a long time. It's just the way things are."

Unsure what else to say, Jake turned back to the window but the view had somehow lost its interest. If indeed it had ever had any, the appeal had faded when the woman across the room has stepped out of his arms. Though she said the words coldly and matter-of-factly, Jake could still almost feel her sadness and loneliness from where he stood several feet away. Any argument he could have rendered would have been negated by his own response to her that one night and he knew it.

Making love to Elizabeth had been a once in a lifetime experience. He knew he'd never forget it. Hell, he'd known that right away. She had been a virgin, inexperienced and innocent and he'd taken advantage of her. Her first time should've been with someone special, someone she loved.

Desperate to put some sort of distance between them, Jake had said as much to her. Her immediate response that she did love him was waved away. A little girl, he'd called her. He winced now, remembering the words he'd said. He'd told her she was too young to know what love was.

When she'd insisted that she loved him, he'd shaken his head. He would never admit it but, she scared him to death. The way it had felt with her...it was like nothing he'd ever known. That was the part that had him worried.

Convincing himself that he was protecting both of them, he had told her that she was a great friend, that she was an amazing girl. He'd reassured her that he loved her. As a friend. What had happened between them wouldn't change that. He would still always be there for her, still be her best friend. But, he'd said, he was not in love with her and just didn't love her that way. He never would.

Neither of them had directly spoken of it since then, trying to pretend it had never happened.

Things had been awkward between them for a bit, but not for long. Nothing ever came between them for long, but damn he regretted those words now.

Absently, he wondered what had possessed him to say those things to her. Fear, he supposed. He'd been afraid of what had happened between them. Terrified of how it had made him feel. It had felt more right than anything he'd done his whole life and it scared the hell out of him.

His actions that night had been far less than noble and he couldn't, to this day, think of anything he could've done that would have been more wrong. And still the way it had felt - holding her, touching her, kissing her. He'd never felt so strongly that it was right and what was supposed to be.

Ever since that night, he'd done his best to forget those feelings and put what had happened between them out of his mind. Only, every time she looked at him, he remembered the wonder and amazement that had filled her eyes. Every time she smiled, he remembered the way her sweet mouth had felt against his. When she touched him, he remembered her timid hands on his body. Even now, when she gave him massages, he remembered. Perhaps that was why he always jumped at the initial contact. She'd touched him a million times since then and it never changed.

He shoved his hands in his pockets and rolled back on his heels for a moment, still contemplating the darkness outside. It seemed to swallow everything, even the happiness he knew existed somewhere in the world. His happiness was Elizabeth though and she wasn't out there. The thought shocked him and he almost ran right at that second, but then took a breath and chalked it up to the situation as well as the late hour.

"Come on, lady," he said softly after a minute, "Let's get you to bed."

# Chapter 5

The next morning, Elizabeth woke up with a horrible headache. The room was spinning and her mouth felt like it was stuffed with cotton. Someone or something was banging quite loudly in her head and the light that streamed in through her window felt like a searing brand as it hit her bleary eyes.

With a small groan, Elizabeth stretched. She froze when her arm met another body. In her bed. There was another person in her bed. *Oh God,* she thought frantically, *what had she done?*

Her eyes spied the short sandy hair and half covered torso and she relaxed. Jake. It was just Jake. Then she froze again. *Jake was in her bed!*

A quick look down had her being flooded with relief once more as she realized that she was fully dressed. Well, she was dressed enough to assure her that nothing had happened that shouldn't have. Her nightshirt and shorts covered all the essentials and Jake had located one of the pairs of sweatpants he'd left at her place on one of the many nights he'd spent.

Elizabeth raised herself up to one elbow and

looked down at the man sleeping by her side. Why had he stayed, she wondered. He looked so relaxed and peaceful, she realized, her mind already distracted from its original train of thought.

She smiled a little as he made a small sound in his sleep and stirred. His hand was flung over his head and his other arm lay across his stomach. The sheet he'd pulled over them lay just south of the waistband of the sweatpants he had donned before bed.

"See anything you like?"

The gravelly, masculine voice startled her while the lazily spoken words made her face flame. She could feel the heat climbing her cheeks as she stammered a noncommittal response. The cocky grin on his face told her he knew exactly what she had been thinking as she had eyed his sleeping form.

Elizabeth made a face at him as she scrambled out of bed, tossing her pillow at his head as she went. She made some comment about guys thinking they could get away with being smartasses just because they were cute. The sound of his chuckle followed her into the bathroom, where she closed the door.

In spite of herself and everything that had happened, she felt a smile coming to her face.

She reached in and twisted the faucets in the shower allowing streams of steamy water into the stall then turned to the medicine cabinet and grabbed a couple of pain pills. A glass of water accompanied them before she pulled the nightshirt over her head and stepped out of her shorts and undies.

A soft tap on the door sent her into a minor panic. Surely, Jake could hear the water and knew she was either in the shower or about to be. Hastily, she grabbed a towel and pulled it across her front before opening the door just the tiniest crack.

Something black and lacy greeted her view through the small gap between the door and frame and she squeaked in mortification. He had brought her underwear! She quickly threw the door open and snapped the undergarments out of his hands. Much to her chagrin, the action merely caused more laughter from the other side of the door.

"You're a dead man, Carpenter!" she promised fiercely when she had safely secured the barrier between them once more.

The chortling from her room told her he wasn't the least bit afraid of her. With mock innocence, he pointed out that he was just being a loving, considerate friend. After all, would she rather come out naked and have to get them herself, not knowing if he was still in the room or not.

Her wildly inappropriate response only served to increase the amount of laughter coming from the other side of the door. His ready agreement to the crude comment made her face flame even more. God, he was horrible!

Another tap on the door had her wondering what more he could possibly want now. This time she wrapped the towel completely around her before releasing the lock and pulling the door open a crack.

Her questioning look was answered by Jake asking if she would prefer waffles, pancakes or French toast for breakfast. One eyebrow ascended slightly as he listed off the options and she wondered if he had even been to her kitchen yet. Apparently not, if he thought she had any of the ingredients to produce such tempting items as he was mentioning. Not to mention the fact that he would have been chewing her out by now if he had seen how little food was actually in her cupboards.

Promising him that they would decide when she finished her shower, she pushed the door shut once more and dropped the towel from her body. She pulled the shower curtain aside and stepped under the water. The slight stinging sensation of the drops pelting her skin woke her up a little more than she had been. Her headache was also starting to recede which was undoubtedly a blessing.

Several long minutes later, she stood in front of the mirror on her medicine cabinet. She pulled a brush through her long damp hair. Now that she had shaved, showered and washed her hair, she felt much more human and alert. She still faintly remembered the events of last night.

With a sigh, she set the brush on the sink and leaned forward, bracing her palms on its cool surface. She remembered everything up until she practically ran out of the restaurant and Jake followed right behind her. The ride to her apartment and everything after that was just a blur.

She very vaguely remembered Jake bringing her into the apartment the night before. There was something about pretending and people leaving her, but it was all so damn foggy. And how had Jake ended up in her bed? He had spent the night at her place countless times, but never once had he slept in her bed with her.

That, she reminded herself, is the reason she never drank. When she did, it was cautiously and she limited her intake severely. She had never seen a point in drinking to get drunk the way other people had.

She had just finished brushing her teeth when she heard Jake call out to her from her bedroom. Her clothes were still in the other room and she would have to go out there to get them, which meant allowing Jake to see her in her under things. That wasn't about to happen.

Instead, she leaned her back against the door and yelled back to him through the wooden obstacle. As she has suspected, he had been in the kitchen already and had returned to fuss at her for her eating habits, or lack thereof. He did that quite often actually, always telling her she didn't take good care of herself.

With an indulgent sigh, she promised she would go out later in the day and get more groceries if he would just go out of her bedroom so she could get dressed. There was a short silence from the other room before he agreed to her terms. After a few seconds, she heard the door between her bedroom and the hallway click closed.

She jerked the door open and hurried to her dresser, quickly grabbing a pair of jeans and a soft knit top that clung lovingly to her curves without being tight. The jeans hugged her rear and she pulled her hair back into a long ponytail at the crown of her head. Satisfied with her appearance, she emerged from the bedroom to find a less than pleased Jake still looking through all her cupboards.

A giggle threatened to escape as she watched him perform the familiar actions he did from time to time. He would open the cupboards and refrigerator and see what little she had. Then, he would proceed to make a list of things he thought she should have on hand and they would argue and discuss and eventually compromise somewhere in the middle between his rather exorbitant requirements and her minimal desires.

Strolling slowly through the living room, Elizabeth came to a stop at the counter that served as a partial divider between the living space and the small cooking area. Grinning cheekily, she crossed her arms and leaned over resting on her elbows. She pretended to mull over the list of items Jake had scrawled onto the notepad she kept on the refrigerator. He had removed it, located a pen and had set it on the counter to enable him to perform his task more easily.

"You're out of coffee," he groused without turning around.

"I know," she replied breezily.

"And milk," he continued.

"Yup," she acknowledged, unperturbed.

"And eggs, bread, meat, juice and pretty much everything. What the hell do you eat?" he growled.

Elizabeth smothered a small smile at the familiarity of the conversation they were having. They had been over it a hundred times before and nothing ever changed. He always threatened that he was going to start buying her groceries for her since she never seemed to remember to do so herself. She would laugh and brush it off, knowing it was an idle if well-intended threat. Granted, he did occasionally bring groceries and juice, but usually just complained about her lack of care where her diet was concerned.

She climbed up on the stool that sat beside the counter and watched as he completed his search of her kitchen. He made a few more entries on his list before putting the pen away removing the top page and returning the magnetized notepad to its rightful place. Turning back toward the counter and Elizabeth, he was just in time to catch the small smirk that still was on her lips.

A slightly raised eyebrow showed her he had noticed and she dutifully pasted a serious expression on her face. From the other side of the counter, he presented her the list he had made, assuming much the same pose she had taken moments before, his arms crossed and resting on his elbows which braced against the cool surface of the countertop. He watched as she perused the small paper and made small comments in agreement or disagreement with a particular item.

When she had finished, she looked up to find Jake watching her intently. A faint flush crept up her cheeks at the dark dangerous hint of purely masculine appreciation in his eyes. She cleared her throat and handed the list back to him, deciding for once to forego the arguing and just go with his request. His stunned expression was almost worth the forthcoming torture of having cookies and other sweets in her home when she tried so hard to avoid them.

She didn't speak but stood and crossed to the door to grab her keys and sneakers. Slipping them on, she tied them quickly while Jake waited patiently. When she straightened, he handed her purse and made a teasing comment about her being so agreeable this morning.

"Yeah, well," she replied. "I figure I have to let you win once in a while."

As he pulled his hand back, Elizabeth's smile

turned to a frown and she reached out. She caught his hand in her own, turning it over. Last night in her state of mind and in the dark, she hadn't noticed the bruising and cut on Jake's knuckles.

"Oh my God!" she exclaimed. "What did you do?"

A slow heat made its way up Jake's neck and into his face. He snatched his hand away and reached for his keys. He'd forgotten all about that.

"Oh, I um, must have hit it on something. Let's go."

"Oh, no you don't," she argued, stopping him. "What happened?"

"I hit something with it. That's all," he reiterated, not quite meeting her eyes. A grim smile stole across his lips in memory of the satisfaction of seeing the other man sprawled out on the floor.

"Jake," she drew out his name, in a tone that told him she knew he wasn't being completely honest. "What exactly did you hit with your hand?"

She had a sneaking suspicion she already knew.

"Well, he called you a ...something not nice," he began.

"What? Who did?" Elizabeth was so confused.

"Mark," he replied nervously.

"Ah, and then he hit your knuckles with his face?" she inquired, raising a brow.

Jake remained silent, unsure if he should admit guilt or if that would merely increase the amount of trouble he was in. She had crossed her arms over her chest and was clearly waiting for his response. Finally, he sighed.

"When you left, I headed out after you and told Allison not to call me anymore and basically they could have each other. Well I'd only taken a few steps when he called out to me. Was telling me he would take you home. He said that since you were his date, you should be leaving with him.

"I disagreed. I told him that you were my best friend and were leaving with me and he needed to never call you or talk to you again. He made a comment about me keeping you to myself and then called you a-" he faltered for a moment, unsure if he should actually repeat the insult.

It was enough for Elizabeth to get the picture though. He'd called her a nasty name and Jake had punched him in the face. She almost felt bad for Mark. Her features softened now as she looked at her best friend.

"Besides, Allison looked pretty peeved when

you two came out of the ladies room, so I know I wasn't the only one who had a little fun causing trouble," he pointed out defensively.

Now it was Elizabeth's face that flamed guiltily. She had been somewhat less than ladylike in her conversation with Jake's girlfriend. Perhaps she should apologize. But her eyes met his and she saw no anger, just a lingering warmth that mirrored what was in her own gaze.

Slowly, Elizabeth reached up and cupped his cheek, kissing his lips briefly. It was the first time she'd ever dared to actually kiss him first since that night, and she had to say she liked it. Still, she kept it brief, pulling back after only a few seconds.

Her eyes met his and she smiled, her thumb stroking his cheek.

"Thank you," she murmured.

Now it was Jake's turn to be confused. He'd expected her to be angry. Instead, she was thanking him.

"For...?" he prompted.

For what, she thought? For being her best friend? For never letting her down? Always being there when she needed him? Defending her? All of it.

"Everything," she smiled and stepped away.

"For just being amazing."

Jake shook his head and followed her down the stairs to his truck and he drove them into town. Elizabeth insisted on stopping for breakfast before heading to the market, pointing out that one should never go grocery shopping on an empty stomach. With an indulgent grin and sigh, he acquiesced and pulled into her favorite pancake house. Even though he knew this was just the start of her procrastination and stalling tactics, he still wore a smile. It was going to be another long day spent with his best friend. What could be better than that?

Sometime later, they had finally accomplished the mission they had set out for that morning. Elizabeth's cupboards, freezer and refrigerator were almost bursting with the purchases they had made. By that time, they were both too tired to put much effort into making dinner, so they agreed that Chinese food and a movie was the way to go.

Hours later, as much as he didn't want to, Jake stood and stretched. He suggested that it was time for him to go home. The smile that had lingered on Elizabeth's lips all day fell away and he felt as if the sun had gone behind the clouds.

As much as he hated to do that, he needed to go home. He needed some time away from her to get his head together, though he used work as an excuse. She was clouding his thinking and he didn't understand why. So he hugged her and went home, even as he wished he could stay the night again.

Jake leaned down for a quick hug and kiss before he walked outside. He waited till he heard the lock click, just like he always did. He liked to make sure she kept her door locked. Once he heard it, he strode toward the stairs and down to the car.

The next morning, Jake opened the door and climbed out of his truck and peered across the street, hoping to catch a glimpse of Elizabeth. He knew she was there because he recognized her car. She was always there bright and early, even on weekends.

He smiled to himself as he entered the station. Elizabeth had worked so hard for everything she had accomplished. There wasn't anyone prouder of her than he was. He knew the long hours and amazing dedication it had taken to get her where she was today.

Jake's friend, Gabe, looked up just long enough to say, "Hey bro" when Jake walked in. He went back to reading his book immediately. Gabe was tall and lean, almost to the point of being skinny. His slight build belied the strength he possessed and many people underestimated him because of it. Some of the guys picked on him but they all knew he could pull his weight.

The thing with being a firefighter was that these people here weren't just coworkers, they were another family. They depended on each other and protected each other. That was just the nature of the job.

They all knew that one small thing going awry could be disastrous. Injuries were sustained, careers cut short, lives ended, every single day. It wasn't something they obsessed over, but something they were aware of with every single call.

His train of thought broke off as the familiar tones sounded, followed by the dispatcher relaying the location of a house on fire. Instantly, everyone flew into motion. Within seconds three crews, two in trucks and one in the ambulance, pulled out of the station.

It took only minutes to reach the burning house. Seconds later, everyone was hurrying around doing their part. They all knew their jobs. An organized chaos fell over the scene as the woman who lived in the house tried to pull Jake aside. Her daughter was still inside.

The paramedics pulled the woman away and Jake followed asking where in the house the child was. He tried hard to understand the mother's hysterical reply. Somewhere in the back of the house was all he could make out though. It was enough for now. He turned away and went to find Gabe and their boss, Kyle.

Kyle was giving instructions, trying to ascertain the location of the blaze. Jake approached and filled them both in and he and Gabe grabbed the equipment they weren't already wearing. A small, water fire extinguisher joined the masks, helmets and air tanks. Then the two men rushed toward the front door.

The smoke instantly pushed them to the floor and they crawled down the hallway as quickly as they could. Smoky darkness made it almost impossible to see as they made their way down the narrow passage. Even through the protective gear they wore, the two men could feel the power of the inferno. The blistering, baking heat threatened to force them back out of the building before they could reach the child.

Jake was always grateful for his thermal imaging camera. It made locating people much easier in the black murkiness that was almost impossible to see through. He could already feel the sweat trickling down his face. This was, without a doubt, as close as a person could get to being in hell, without actually dying.

Suddenly, there in front of him was a doorway. Jake hoped against hope that it was the room that held the girl they were searching for. The camera told him it was. Before he knew it, the child was in his arms. Gabe led the way back outside as Jake cradled the unconscious toddler and crawled back toward the front door.

Then they were outside. The cool outside air was a stark contrast to the withering heat inside. Jake could hear the relieved sobs and screams of the mother as she saw him carry her daughter quickly to the waiting ambulance. As he approached, two of the paramedics who had been waiting met him and took the child from his arms.

Before he could take two steps, the woman barreled into him, throwing her arms around him and squeezing him with a surprising strength. Over and over again, she thanked him for saving her baby. He steadied her with one arm as he guided her into the back of the ambulance where the paramedics already had the girl on oxygen.

Jake shut the door behind her and gave two solid raps to signal the driver to leave. Instantly, the vehicle sped away, lights and sirens going. The girl would be fine, he told himself, even as he knew he lied. He knew she wasn't breathing when he'd held her close to him. He could only hope she hadn't been without oxygen for too long, that she hadn't been burned too badly for her little body to recover. Now, he forced himself to turn his attention to the rest of his job, getting the fire put out.

Jake reentered the house and joined the firefighters who were manning the hose, aiming the stream of water at the blaze. The heat of the flames was an almost palpable force, threatening to scorch every man in the building. Steam filled the air as the water evaporated in the unbelievable heat.

It only took about ten minutes to extinguish the flames. Finishing up the call was another matter. After the fire was out, it took another hour or two to move debris around, looking for any hotspots. Occasionally, even though the actual flames were out, it could continue to smolder and if those smoldering areas weren't caught and extinguished, it could flare back up again.

Jake and a couple of the other firefighters took their axes and other tools around and smashed into the ceiling and walls to be sure there was nothing missed. They were nothing if not thorough. Last thing they wanted was to have something start burning again. From there it was all up to the investigators who would come in and determine the cause and origin of the fire. Jake's job was done.

# Chapter 6

Elizabeth stepped into the relative dimness of the gym from outside. Jake was there, just as she'd known he would be. His face was red with exertion, sweat pouring off of him and still he was giving the heavy bag a thrashing that made her almost pity the inanimate object.

She had gone looking for him when he didn't show up at her place like he was supposed to. They had talked the night before and decided they would have dinner. He was going to meet her at her place and they were going to the steakhouse she liked. That was two hours ago.

Sometimes, when he'd had a bad day, he would go to the gym to work off his emotions. Normally, she'd let him be, knowing that sometimes he just needed his space. But tonight, she came to him. Damned if she could explain it but something was telling her that this time, he needed her. Not that he would ever admit that.

She had told him on many occasions that, if he ever needed to talk, she was there. He'd only taken her up on the offer a couple of times, when there had been particularly bad calls. She still remembered with vivid clarity, the ones he'd talked to her about.

One had been a call where some kids has stolen a car and gone joy riding. The car had crashed into a pole, killing two of them. He'd had to work around their bodies to help the third kid in the back seat. That one had stuck with him for years and she shuddered with the memory of just him telling her. There was no way she could have handled that, she knew. Jake had admitted that it had been more than a little challenging for him as well. Trying to pretend he wasn't working around two dead human beings had been damn near impossible.

"The thing is," he'd told her, "You know that just a few moments before, those people were alive. They were laughing, talking, and enjoying life. Then, they're just...gone. There was nothing I could do. I didn't even have a chance of saving them. And to try to forget they were there-" he'd broken off then.

He'd never finished that thought, but there had been no need. Elizabeth had gotten the picture all too well. Things like that could scar a man, and this man bore many scars. Too bad most people didn't see them.

The only other one he'd been bothered enough to talk to her about was one involving a little boy, his father and grandfather. They had been in their front yard and a passerby had lost control of their car, sending it flying over a guardrail and into the yard where the trio had been enjoying the evening. All three of them had ultimately succumbed to their injuries, but he'd remembered working on the father as they sped toward the hospital. He'd told her he knew the man wasn't going to make it when each chest compression he performed, only made the man's wounds bleed more. Still, he'd tried. He had worked on that man until the hospital staff took over upon arrival. Another scar nobody would ever see. Except her.

Elizabeth knew he'd shown her a side of himself that few would ever glimpse. He'd trusted her enough to show those rare moments of vulnerability. Somehow, that made him even stronger in her eyes.

Until he'd opened up and talked to her about those, Elizabeth, like most people, had thought she knew what it meant to be a firefighter and paramedic. She'd understood the death, the violence, the blood and everything else. Even the danger she'd known about. After all, he'd been burned once too. Nothing serious, just singed his ears, but it was enough to fuel her fears. Then, after she'd heard these stories, she'd realized she still had no clue. Even though she'd never told Jake, hearing those things had made it so Elizabeth worried about him even more. Some nights, when Jake was working, she didn't sleep.

She wondered now if this would be the third call she would hear about. There was no doubt in her mind that something at work was the reason that she had had to come find him here. It was just a matter of whether or not Jake would actually talk to her about it.

It was a few moments before he noticed she was there, lost in his own world. His eyes met hers across the room and he paused in his abuse of the swinging object in front of him. Using both hands, he caught it and stilled it before reaching for the towel he had tossed on the floor about an hour before.

Removing the gloves he'd donned before abusing the heavy bag, he mopped his face with the towel as he strode across the room, weaving his way between machines and the people using them. She never came here. The fact that she was here now concerned him. Had something happened? He'd left his phone in the locker room. Maybe she'd tried to call.

Even on normal days, a workout after work didn't hurt to help blow off steam. Today was different. It was always harder when there was there was a child involved. It was even harder when he didn't know that the child was going to make it. There was no telling how long she had not been breathing when he got to her.

He knew there was nothing more he could have done. In his heart, he knew it wasn't his fault. And none of that meant a damn thing because a baby was fighting for her life now. A thousand "if onlys" ran through his head. If only the woman had checked the batteries in the smoke alarm. If only they had been there a couple minutes earlier.

Now none of those things mattered. It was done. Nothing he did or said or felt could change it and damn it, he hated that!

He'd checked with the medics who had taken the girl to the hospital and found out they'd been able to get her breathing on her own again before they arrived. Of course, they couldn't tell him what the long term prognosis was but knowing she'd been breathing on her own was a good thing. He tried to focus on that as he walked over to Elizabeth.

"Hey fella," she murmured as he approached. "You okay?"

"Yeah," he lied tightly, forcing a smile.

"Bull," she retorted without heat. "You're a lousy liar."

"Why are you here?" he asked.

"You were supposed to be at my place two hours ago," she reminded him.

Jake's eyes met Elizabeth's and she saw the guilt, pain and worry in their depths. She didn't know what, but something had happened at work that left him upset. Sooner or later she would hear about it, but for now, she would just offer her support.

"Damn. I'm sorry, I forgot."

"I know," she waved off his apology lightly. "How about some dinner?" she asked softly.

Jake shook his head. She bothered him in so many ways. He was sure spending time around Elizabeth would only confuse things further.

"I don't-" he began.

"Come on," she urged, gently, "You promised."

Jake sighed and nodded, "Yeah, ok. I need a shower."

"Ok, I can wait here if you want. Unless you'd rather go home."

"No it's ok. I'll just be a couple minutes."

She reached for him and he shied away, explaining he didn't want to get her sweaty. Elizabeth scoffed at the objection and hugged him tight for a moment, asking when she had ever cared about that. Jake sighed as he returned the embrace. Her simple warm touch was the soothing balm he needed but hadn't been able to obtain. An hour on the heavy bag hadn't done as much as the feel of her arms around him.

Unable to help himself, he buried his face in her hair, inhaling the scent that always seemed like a balm for his heart. One last deep breath and he dropped a quick kiss on the top of her head. Then he pushed himself away, heading to the showers.

Although Elizabeth had originally intended to still go to the steak house to eat, they ended up eating at her place again. She stopped and picked up some pizza and they went back home to eat it. There wasn't as much conversation as normal given Jake's mood but they both were ok with that. They spent several hours just sitting on the couch together relaxing and enjoying each other's company.

Finally, Jake shifted and said he guessed he should think about getting home. It was getting late.

"You could stay the night," she offered.

Jake hesitated. He'd spent countless nights at her apartment, and she at his. But that was before. Now, Things were starting to get more and more difficult where she was concerned. He was feeling things he'd sworn he would never feel again, and not for her at least.

"I don't know," he began, trying to find an easy way to deny her request.

"I have food now," she added in a singsong voice, "I could make breakfast in the morning. I could even make coffee!"

Jake laughed a little and started to shake his head, "Sorry honey. I don't know that I could take a night on your couch tonight."

Elizabeth frowned and bit her lip, hesitating before voicing her next thought. "You could um, sleep with me again…"

Jake froze. Did she have any bloody clue what she was saying? Sleeping next to her the other night had been a special blend of heaven and hell rolled into one. The warmth of her soft body snuggled close to him had been a pleasure like he'd seldom known. At the same time, her succulent curves had made sleeping damn near impossible, arousing him beyond reason.

He'd known damn well that would be the case when he'd decided to stay with her. It had been against his better judgment to do so but he'd been unable to refuse her request. He'd been about to walk out of her room when he'd barely discerned the softly spoken plea to not leave her. How could he not do as she asked?

"Elizabeth, I – " he started to say and stopped

at the disappointment on her face. Damn it! What the hell. Couldn't get any worse, he reasoned to himself. "Okay, I'll stay."

Moments later, both of them had showered and changed for bed. Jake was dressed again in a pair of sweats that he kept at her place. He was more than thankful that she had at least had enough pity on him to cover most of her tantalizing skin. A short sleeved pajama shirt topped the pants that covered her from waist to ankle.

Until a few nights ago, he had never actually slept in bed with her. He couldn't help feeling a little awkward as he climbed into bed next to her. As soon as she snuggled close, all awkwardness disappeared and he wondered how something that seemed wrong could feel so right. This was Elizabeth for crying out loud! How could holding her in bed feel as if it was the most natural thing in the world?

He sighed to himself and gave up trying to figure it out as she left his arms long enough to shut off the bedside lamp. She settled back against him and he absently stroked her side. They lay silently in the dark for a few moments, before Elizabeth spoke, almost startling him.

"How do you do it?" she asked out of the blue.

Jake shook his head slightly, having no clue what in the world she was talking about. How did he do what?

"How do you do what you do every day I mean? Be a firefighter and a medic? How do you go to call after call, never knowing what's waiting? How do you deal with getting there and knowing you're too late?"

They'd talked occasionally about his work but she'd never asked anything like that before. He considered for a moment before answering. It wasn't something he'd ever really thought about. It was just what he did.

"I don't honestly know. I just...do" he shrugged. "It's like...I don't know. I don't have a choice. It is what it is and it's who I am. I can't change it, so I just do what I can to save the ones who can be saved."

"But doesn't it get to you?" she pressed.

"Of course it does. It's never easy to get there and know I can't help. Especially if it's a child. It never gets easier to tell a parent their kid is dead. Usually, it's something that could have been prevented. I don't want to say that if they hadn't turned their back, their baby wouldn't have fallen in the pool and drowned. I never want to tell them if they had just been a damn parent like they were supposed to, their kid would still be alive. Sometimes, I want to lie and say yes your baby will be fine. But I can't. So yes, sometimes, it's hard."

"How do you deal with working on someone and losing them anyway?"

He paused for another moment, considering her question silently.

"It's hard sometimes. I'm not really religious or anything but a lot of times it kind of helps to just think that that's just the way God intended it. It was just their time. I just have to remind myself that I did all I could do. Sometimes it works, sometimes it doesn't."

"You know sometimes, don't you?" she inquired, her voice barely above a whisper.

Jake paused for a moment, not quite sure what she meant. Elizabeth turned sleepily to face him, tipping her chin up as if she were looking at him. There was no way she could see his expression though, not as dark as it was in the room.

Then she clarified, "You know sometimes when you go on a call. You know they're going to die don't you? That no matter what you do, it's not going to be enough?"

Jake stiffened slightly. She'd hit one of the few nerves he had when talking about his work. He'd always been a sore loser. Death was no exception. He had a very hard time losing to the bastard. Still, it was a part of his job. There was no escaping that. As much as he may wish at times that he was God, and could fix everything with a touch, it just wasn't going to be. It was difficult to accept that but, that was the reality.

"Yeah," his answer was shorter than he'd intended and she wondered if she'd angered him by asking.

"But you still try," she pressed. It was a statement, not a question. She couldn't help it. Her curiosity was getting the better of her.

"You still try and give it your all. You pour every bit of yourself into it. Even though you know it won't help."

She felt rather than heard his affirmative grunt. He wasn't sure he liked where this conversation was going. There was no ill will behind her questions and he knew that, but he wasn't used to talking about this stuff and to do so now was taking him into territory he wasn't comfortable with.

"Why?"

Jake hesitated again, unsure how to answer. He mulled it over in his mind for a few moments. Elizabeth remained still against him in the darkness. When he spoke it was slowly and softly.

"I have to. Even if it wasn't an actual requirement of the job itself, I'd have to. There's someone I have to answer to, every day. Someone to whom I am accountable for every decision, every action. And every lack of action. It's more than just being able to tell the family I tried. This man is in the mirror every morning and I can't avoid him. He's very demanding and unforgiving. In order to meet his eyes every day, to be able to look him in the face, I can't do anything less. There's always a chance, until there's not. Yes, sometimes I know there's no way in hell I can save them. But I can't not try. I can't justify anything less than an all out effort.

Even doing that, there are always a thousand, no a million, 'What if?' questions. Could I have done something different? Was there another way to save them that I didn't think of? And that's when I do absolutely everything I can. At least if I know I have pushed the envelope, done everything humanly possible, that I can face that man in the morning with my head held high. I know I can tell him I gave it my all."

He felt her slight nod on his arm, and almost heard her mind working as she pondered his answer. Then, she nodded again and he heard her breathing slow and deepen.

"Sleep now," he whispered. "I'll be here."

And with that they both drifted off.

# Chapter 7

October twentieth arrived before Elizabeth could believe it. It was the day of Nick and Kate's long-awaited wedding. She never had been a morning person but for her friend she had made an exception, dragging herself out of bed at an ungodly hour to get hair done, and makeup on and dressed to the nines. For Katie, she was even wearing heels.

The church was filled to capacity with family and friends who had turned up to witness the ceremony. Flowers and ribbon adorned basically every surface they had been able to access and there had never been a more beautiful wedding, Elizabeth was sure. As she helped the younger woman with the final touch preparations, she was also sure there had never been a more beautiful bride.

Katie was practically glowing, eager to march down the aisle and marry the man of her dreams. Elizabeth felt a small twinge of envy, which she quickly squelched. She wished she were even close to marrying the man she loved, but realistically, she stood more of a chance of winning the lottery than marrying anyone at all within the foreseeable future.

The moment was close and Brad came in to see if Katie was ready to go. She nodded and Elizabeth picked up the small bouquet she would carry. Hugging Katie, she scurried out the door and waited behind the big double doors with the flower girl and her mother.

Finally, the door opened and organ music filled the air. Automatically, her eyes searched for Jake. There he was, up at the altar right at his brother's side. Their gazes locked and Elizabeth felt her heart pound against her ribs.

With every step, she reminded herself that she was not walking toward Jake. She was not the one whose dreams were coming true today. Jake was not going to take her hand when she reached her destination.

Jake felt his breath catch as Elizabeth appeared at the back of the church. God, but she was beautiful. The silver sheath she wore fit snugly, accentuating every feminine curve on her body. Her copper curls were caught up in some sort of fancy style that he couldn't have named if he tried and only a few locks were left to frame her delicate features.

Even from a distance, he could see the light of

her eyes and he had to force himself to breathe. For whatever reason, he was having the hardest time remembering that she was not walking to him. The closer she came, the harder his heart raced in his chest.

Finally, she turned away from him, assuming her place on the opposite side of the altar and lowered her eyelids, shielding her gaze from him. He wondered if she was thinking along the same lines as he was, or if he was just totally and completely insane. That was probably the case, he convinced himself.

The music changed and everyone turned their attention to the rear of the room once more. Brad and Katie appeared where Elizabeth had been moments before and Jake tried to focus his attention on the pair now making their way closer. Of their own volition, his eyes returned to Elizabeth and he was only mildly surprised to find her already watching him. Her face colored slightly before she returned her attention to the bride, where his own should be.

Elizabeth listened absently to the preacher as he began reciting the familiar words. It was just the atmosphere of the wedding, she told herself. They always made her think this way, wistful and weepy. It would only last a few more minutes, she reminded herself sternly. Then would come the fun part, the dancing, laughing, eating, drinking. She could last a few more minutes.

It was a few hours later, however, that she searched Jake out at the reception. The party had been going for quite some time, but he'd disappeared a while ago. She found him now, leaning against the rail of the deck overlooking the water.

They couldn't have picked a better place to hold a reception, Elizabeth thought to herself. The restaurant backed onto a big lake and the rail Jake rested on now was partly for looks and partly to prevent people falling in the water. It was a beautiful view though, water as far as the eyes could see. To her, it seemed like something from a book or a movie, as she came up to her friend.

Jake heard the footsteps approach and knew Elizabeth had found him. He had known she would. She somehow seemed to have a sixth sense for when something was bothering him and always made herself available to help. Any second now, he expected to feel the gentle touch of her hand on his back or his arm.

Instead, he was surprised to see her take up a pose much like the one he was holding, just a few inches away. Her arms crossed, she rested her elbows on the same piece of wood his own occupied. She leaned forward, her sight fixed on some imaginary point out over the water.

Neither of them spoke for a moment, content to enjoy the view and each other's company. Jake could tell she had something on her mind, though, and he knew she was aware that he did too. It was as if there were some unspoken contest to see which of them would break the silence first.

As the silence lengthened, he glanced over at her, unable to help himself. The sunset was reflecting off the water, shining on her face with the ever changing motion of the waves. He couldn't help noticing the swell of her breasts above the bodice as she stood there, waiting. They were both waiting now.

Finally, she couldn't take it anymore. He'd known she would be the first to speak. She wouldn't let it go too long, knowing something was up.

"You disappeared," she said at last.

"I needed some air," he replied, knowing she wouldn't let it go at that.

"You're lying to me," she stated baldly, her green eyes finally catching his.

He should have known better than to try to pull one over on her. But, damn it, he had no idea how to even begin to tell her what he was thinking! How could he explain it to her, when he couldn't even make sense of it himself?

"Just...weddings. You know," he gestured vaguely in the direction of the crowd behind them.

She nodded wordlessly, her gaze still pinned to his.

"It just makes me think...things," he finished somewhat lamely, turning his face back toward the lake.

"Like that it could have been us?" she offered, and his head snapped up.

They stayed like that for a moment, motionless. Each seemed to be challenging the other in a moment of truth neither would admit had been coming. Jake had suspected their thoughts were running on the same parallel but to have it confirmed out loud was something else.

After what seemed an eternity, he nodded.

"Yeah," he acknowledged, his voice deeper than normal.

Elizabeth looked away, determined not to meet his eyes lest he see the pain the next words brought her. But she knew, even though he'd said nothing, that they accompanied the thoughts they'd just voiced. It wasn't a shock.

But it still was hard to say them.

"But there are so many reasons it can't be us, aren't there, Jake?" she asked, her voice choked.

Jake nodded, knowing she couldn't see him. While he couldn't look away from her, she seemed to be intentionally avoiding looking at him. There were many reasons, but standing here with her now, he was damned if he could recall a single one.

It was a full minute probably before Elizabeth finally nodded and straightened. She drew a deep breath and turned to go, never looking at him directly. Was he imagining it or were her eyes misting over?

"Catch you later, fella," she mumbled before hurrying away as fast as the heels would let her.

She had never been one for wearing dress shoes and Jake wasn't at all surprised to see her stop to remove them before practically running away. His instincts, not to mention his heart, screamed at him to go after her. But his brain, far louder than the other two, won out with its insistence to stay put.

Elizabeth stumbled through the throng of well wishers, looking for Nick and Katie. She would plead a headache and head home. The desire to stay and celebrate their union had deserted her and now she just wanted to be alone.

At last, she found them. Pasting the brightest smile on her face that she could scrounge up, she hugged them both tightly and made her apologies. Nick frowned as she spoke though and asked her what was really wrong. He, like his older brother, was far too perceptive at times. This was one of those times.

Elizabeth looked up, intent on convincing him that it truly was just a headache. The sight of Jake just a few feet away though, stopped that notion in its tracks and Elizabeth blinked hard, shaking her head. She backed away from Nick, mumbling some reaffirmation of her previous excuse, her eyes never leaving the man just over Nick's shoulder.

Nick's eyes followed Elizabeth's departure for a moment, knowing she had just lied through her teeth. Something was bothering her. Her eyes had that weepy look she could never quite conceal. Following a hunch, he turned his head and found his brother watching her leave as well.

Jake. Of course. Something was going on with the two of them, Nick knew. Even though both of them denied it, something was definitely up.

Nick paused for a second, whispering in Katie's ear and giving her a quick kiss. Then, he determinedly strode toward his older brother.

Jake didn't even see him until Nick cleared his throat. He was so caught up in watching the redhead's departure that he hadn't even noticed Nick's presence.

"So, what the hell did you do or say to Elizabeth, Jake?" Nick questioned accusingly.

Jake looked away guiltily. In all honesty, he knew he'd done nothing wrong. The feeling in his gut called him a liar. He never had, and never would, willingly cause Elizabeth pain. In fact, he had and would, go to extensive lengths to prevent it. Now, though, he'd done just that. He knew it was his fault.

As much as he wanted to blame it on the wedding, the atmosphere, the circumstances, he knew it was him. He was afraid of Elizabeth. He was afraid of loving her, of wanting her. No, he corrected himself, he was afraid of losing her.

"Nothing," Jake muttered finally, hoping the brusque tone would discourage further questioning. "We're fine."

His brother looked at him, a little too knowingly.

"She didn't look 'fine' to me, Jake."

"No, I know. I just - just let it go Nick. It'll work itself out."

Even as he said the words, Jake fervently hoped he was right. He'd never given Elizabeth false hope, never led her to believe there was anything more than friendship between them. Now, he had to hope he hadn't lost even that.

The day of Jake's move arrived with annoyingly bright sunshine waking Elizabeth far earlier than she would've liked. She usually kept the drapes closed to keep the sun from waking her, allowing her the luxury of sleeping in on the weekends. The east facing window caught the sun full on each morning, making staying asleep after dawn no easy task.

Today though, she looked at the clock and swore. She was supposed to be at Jake's in five minutes. Damn, she should've set an alarm.

She had just finished in the shower and was pulling on a pair of old comfortable blue jeans when her cell phone rang. Snapping it up off the sink, she stared at the display a moment, forcing her still bleary eyes to focus enough to discern that Jake was the caller. No doubt, he wanted to know where she was. It was only ten minutes after she was supposed to be there but she was never late.

She told him she was leaving in about thirty seconds. After hanging up the phone, she looked in the mirror, pulling a brush quickly through her thick curly hair. With little regard to style or comfort, and far more attention to speed, she grabbed up a hair elastic on her way out of the small bathroom.

She checked to be sure she had her phone in her pocket as she hurried through the apartment, grabbing her shoes and slipping them on quickly. Next stop was her keys and a quick look around the apartment for her purse. She hated that damn thing and would have quite happily given it up if she didn't need to carry so much. Her wallet and a few female necessities took up most of the space in the small bag that was all she would carry.

Yanking it off the table, she all but slammed the door behind her and took the steps two at a time. A small, wry smile touched her lips as she went. Jake would have chewed her out if he could see her running down the steps like that. He was always so worried about her. Even when he was away, he would call or text often to be sure she was ok.

The only time she could remember ever being out of touch with him for more than a day or two at a time was when she had gone away. Her clear eyes clouded with the painful memory she tried to banish whenever it surfaced. She pushed it away once more, climbing into her car and pressing the accelerator to the floor.

Her mind wandered as she drove and she let

it this time. Far more pleasant memories filled her thoughts now. A faint smile touched her face as she remembered. She'd been out of town at a massage therapist's conference and had gotten a late start back. It was about five in the morning when she ended up slipping off the road in the snow. Another car had lost control and was headed straight for her. In her swerving effort to avoid the impending collision, her car had just gone off the edge of the road.

The car had been unharmed as had she, but she had been unable to get the vehicle out of the ditch herself in the dark. Jake had made her promise to call him when she got back home, no matter what time it was. Since she knew she wouldn't be making it home without some kind of divine intervention, she had decided to give him a call just as a heads up, rather than have him wake in the morning and not have received a call from her.

His sleepy, sexy voice had answered on the second ring, instantly perking up when he'd recognized who the caller was. She'd had to assure him at least a dozen times that she was ok, before he finally believed her. Though she should have known better to begin with, she told him she would be fine till daybreak when she could actually see something and get herself out.

Jake, however, would have none of it.

He'd insisted she tell him where she was as near as possible. Then, he'd promised to be there as soon as he could. And he had. About an hour later, she'd dimly seen the headlights of his truck through the swirling snow and had smiled at the notion that it was a real life knight in shining armor scenario. He was coming to the rescue of a damsel in distress.

Although he had been nothing but pleasant and relieved that she appeared to be unhurt, he had not seen the amusement in the situation. He had greeted her with his usual hug and kiss on the cheek and never once said a word about being dragged out of bed to come save her. Not even in the years since the incident, although now it was kind of a standing joke between them.

Pulling her thoughts back to the present, Elizabeth pulled up in front of Jake's apartment. She could see the moving van he'd rented from where she sat and watched for a moment as he carried a box down the stairs and into the van. Evidently, he'd already been up and working for quite some time as sweat beaded on his forehead and lent his skin a glowing sheen in the bright sunlight. An exasperated sigh escaped her as she shook her head at her own folly.

They hadn't spoken much since the wedding and she was still a little upset, though logically, she knew she shouldn't be. She had no right whatsoever to be disappointed, hurt or any of the other emotions she'd been feeling the past week. No matter how many times she told her heart that, though, it refused to listen to reason. Now, though, as she watched her friend, those thoughts melted away and all she wanted was to be near him again.

He had, at some point, removed his shirt and she watched the play of hard muscle under his skin as he moved. In spite of herself, she couldn't help staring. Damn, but that man was built. She knew well how strong his arms were when they held her close. The lean hips were so powerful when he was- Elizabeth cut the thought off abruptly. That was the absolute last thing she needed to be thinking about right now.

She stepped out of the car. Her long, graceful stride carried her over to the van where she waited for him to reappear. She rested her shoulder against the wall of the truck, smothering a small smile at the sight of him bent over, placing the large box in between two others of equal size.

When he straightened and turned, he caught sight of her and an answering smile crossed his lips.

"So," she began with a teasing lilt to her soft, silky tone. "Are all the guys here as good looking as you are?"

He chuckled as he reached over and hugged her tight.

"Not even close," he replied with assumed haughtiness that made her grin again.

She hugged him back, only mildly surprised when he brushed her mouth with his lips. The caress was quick and over before it began. Still, it was enough to set her heart racing as he always did.

Arms around each other's waists, they made their way over to the stairs to continue emptying what they could out of Jake's apartment. They laughed and talked throughout the morning as they took box after box of his possessions out to the van. Some of the stuff still had not been boxed up yet and Jake apologized for that.

Elizabeth waved off his apology, asking what she could do to help. He nodded down the hall toward his bedroom where, aside from the living room, were the only items remaining to be relocated to a box. Jake explained that there were only a few things left that he hadn't gotten to yet and Elizabeth nodded her understanding.

"You can go down there and pack that stuff

up for me if you want," he said.

Elizabeth's heart jumped into her throat and she did her best to stifle the reaction. As close as they had been and as long as they had known each other, she had never been in his bedroom except to sleep. Even as a grown woman now, she wasn't quite sure how she felt about wandering into uncharted territory, touching his things and boxing them up. He had given permission in asking her assistance, but still it seemed awkward somehow.

It took her a minute to realize that Jake was looking at her oddly. There was another minute before she realized that her face was as hot as the sunshine outside at the thought of being in his private space. She should have known she couldn't hide her uneasiness at the idea.

"You don't have to," he offered. "You can stay out here and do this and I can go take care of that if it bothers you for some reason."

Elizabeth shook her head briefly, stepping toward the room in question.

"It's ok. I can do it."

"Elizabeth?" he called.

Her eyes met his questioningly.

"You're not nervous about going into my bedroom are you?" a small smile was struggling to break free on his face and she knew it.

With as much disdain as she could muster, she denied the accusation, lifted her chin and turned on her heel. She faltered as she reached his doorway though and paused for half a second before forcing herself to enter the room. An odd feeling crept over her as she crossed the threshold to the place Jake had slept so many nights.

*Don't be stupid,* she thought to herself, sternly. Many times, she had spent the night in his bed. He'd been in her room. She had even slept in the same bed with him, more than once. The fact that she would be actually going through his things and touching his clothes was irrelevant.

The room was mostly empty, the bed having already been dismantled and moved off to the side. A deep breath, intended to steady herself, instead brought her the heady male scent she knew was only Jake's. She knew it was useless to steel herself against the effects it had on her body, but still she tried.

"You sure you want to do this?" a voice behind her startled her and she nearly jumped out of her skin.

She uttered a four letter word that had her face instantly red with mortification and Jake's with laughter. The tall, muscular form doubled over with the strength of his guffaws and

Elizabeth narrowed her eyes at him. Her face clearly said that while he was amused by her reaction, he had better watch himself because payback was hell.

Looking around the room, her eyes lit on one of the few articles still littering the almost bare floor. A pillow would do nicely, she decided and raced for it before she could change her mind. The blow caught Jake completely off guard and his expression was so comical that this time, it was Elizabeth who was unable to control her giggles.

Even as Jake moved with false menace slowly into the room, Elizabeth kept laughing. Before she knew what was happening, he had grabbed the other pillow and they were engaged in an all out pillow fight. She hadn't done that since she was a little girl, if then.

Though Jake played nice, keeping his swings gentle in nature, he still managed to knock Elizabeth just enough off balance that she couldn't remain upright. He reacted quickly, dropping his pillow, grabbing her around the waist and turning so he broke her fall. A slight grunt accompanied the impact as their bodies landed.

Still laughing slightly, Elizabeth felt the full length of her body in intimate contact with

Jake's and the laughter faded. So close she could see the tiny flecks of amber within his eyes, Elizabeth felt her throat tighten. Jake's arms were still around her, his hands absently stroking up and down her back.

Involuntarily, she moved her hips against him, drawing out a small groan from his throat. Her body shifted again and his hands stilled her hips. God, it was the sweetest, cruelest form of torture.

Her sweetness was just as tempting now as it had been all those years ago. He wanted more than anything to bury himself in her again. He needed to feel that sweet surrender of her body yielding to his. Elizabeth squirmed against him again and threatened the single thread of control he had left.

"You're playing with fire, honey," he warned, his voice a dangerously low growl.

Unable to resist temptation, Elizabeth egged him on. She relaxed her arms slightly allowing their bodies into even more intimate contact than they already were. Her efforts paid off as she watched a flash of raw hunger pass over him.

"I'm a big girl, Jake," she murmured throatily. "I can take the heat."

God, but she was making this hard. In more ways than one. Was she trying to drive him insane?

"Besides," she continued, feigning innocence as her fingers lazily trailed over his arms, "You're a fireman. I'm pretty sure you can put out any fires that may come up."

She slid her fingers between them, raising herself just enough to allow her fingertips to feel the heated skin of his belly. That was all it took. Next thing she knew, she was under Jake and he was kissing her hungrily. His mouth was gentle but insistent on her own and she met his demands eagerly. The hard proof of his desire burned against her thigh almost driving her mad.

Of its own volition, her body arched toward his, pressing her even closer against him. Jake obviously didn't mind as he tightened his grip and slid one jean-clad leg between her thighs. She couldn't help her body's reaction as her hips ground against the hardness of his thigh.

A groan escaped him, answering her own as the air between them heated even more. One of Jake's hands found its way to her breast, teasing the nipple into a hardened peak and drawing a gasp of pleasure from Elizabeth's lips. He raised himself slightly to look down into the flaming green eyes that had snapped open at the touch of his hand on the sensitive skin.

Hesitantly, Elizabeth slid her own hands up between them again to feel the warm taut skin of his belly once more. She encountered a light dusting of hair as her hands slid further up covering his chest and eliciting another groan. The hardness against her thigh was making her crazy. She needed to feel him inside her. Now.

Elizabeth made an instant decision, shutting out all the voices in her head screaming that it was a mistake. She raised her arms over her head, indicating to Jake that he should remove her shirt. When he hesitated, she ground herself against him once more, demanding silently what she could not voice aloud.

Jake closed his eyes tight, his jaw clenching with the effort of reining himself in. He wanted her so bad right now. It would be so easy to accept what she was offering, to remove her clothes and slide inside her and give in to what they both wanted so badly. But that honor of his was rearing its ugly head and whispering that he couldn't take advantage of her like that again.

There were rules. The number one rule was don't get involved with Elizabeth. He'd been with several women, but Elizabeth was off limits. He would screw it up. Elizabeth deserved better.

She was losing him. Elizabeth could see it in

his eyes when he opened them once more. Disappointment made her eyes sting and she turned her head to the side as she fought the urge to cry. Jake moved to the side and sat up, pulling Elizabeth with him.

She shook her head and bit her lip in silent confusion. What was so wrong with her that he wouldn't let himself be with her? Had she been so inept that he couldn't bring himself to be with her like that again?

She had no idea she had spoken out loud until Jake's startled, "What?!" echoed through the nearly empty room like a gunshot.

God, she'd done it again, thrown herself at him. And this time, he'd rejected her. Elizabeth chewed her lip some more and averted her gaze, turning away. Jake was having none of it though and turned her face back to his.

"Is that what you think?" he demanded, stunned.

The rapid blinking of her eyes and continued silence were all the answer he needed. Hell, that is what she thought. She honestly thought he didn't want her. Even worse, she thought it was because she hadn't been good the first time.

"My god, honey, do you really think that's true?"

This time, a small nod was her reply and he

could tell she was struggling to maintain control. A few choice four letter words ran through his mind at the realization of what had been going through her head. Most of those words and a few more were directed at himself for not picking up on it before.

He jammed a hand through the little hair he had on his head, at a loss for what to do or say. Then, he grabbed her and pulled her into his lap against her resistance. With a deep sigh, he cradled her against his chest for a moment, mulling over what to say to make her see that this was not the case and still not reveal the depth of his feelings for her.

"Do you really not know? Do you not see it?" the confused look on her face told him no more clearly than if she'd spoken the word aloud.

She had no idea that he struggled every day not to kiss her. Every time he saw her, he had to resist the urge to take her in his arms. Whenever they spent the night at each other's house, it was damn near impossible to not go down the hall and make her his once more. She had no clue.

"To hell with it," he ground out at last and tipped her face up to his once more.

Their mouths met and all gentleness was gone. Only fire and hunger were in his kiss this time. No teasing this time, his kiss seared her to her soul and she responded in kind, abandoning all pretense of control.

The need was urgent now and she could feel it in the way he touched her. Even though he forced himself to maintain some semblance of gentleness, the raw need was evident in his manner. His hands almost tore the shirt from her body, exposing her breasts to the cool air in the room and the heat of his eyes.

Before she could cover herself, his lips claimed one taut peak, suckling in a way that drove her to the edge of insanity before he moved to the other nipple to do the same. While his mouth pulled on her breasts, forcing an almost continuous moan from her mouth, his hand worked its way down her body and found the waistband of her jeans. Her skin was so warm, so sweet. God, he wanted to bury himself inside her and stay there forever.

His teeth caught one small nipple before soothing it with his tongue. Elizabeth groaned again, thinking the man was going to drive her insane. She arched against him again, biting her tongue to fight the urge to plead with him to end the torment. As sweet as it was, she wanted him now.

One of Jake's hands tangled in her hair and he tugged slightly, not enough to hurt, just enough to tip her head back. The move allowed him open access to the long, pale column of her throat and he buried his face there, his teeth grazing the skin. Instantly, his lips kissed it better, drawing another moan from her as his hands made their way to her waist.

Jake's nimble fingers made quick work of the button and zipper holding the jeans on her body. He reached inside to touch her most sensitive place. A startled cry of pleasure was his reward as he teased and rubbed the flesh he had found. When he slid a finger inside her, she tightened before her entire body seemed to explode with the pleasure and she cried out her release.

He smiled in spite of himself at hearing his name repeatedly whispered from her lips. She couldn't say anything else and he knew that. That was what he was trying for after all.

After the explosion had rocked her body and subsided, he lay her back on the floor and removed her jeans quickly but carefully. Then he stood and removed his own clothing with much more speed and far less care. He paused only a moment to grab a small foil packet from his pocket before rejoining her on the floor.

Taking a second to protect her, he knelt between her thighs for an instant. The next moment, he was filling her. She bit her lip to contain a cry of delight. With one long steady stroke, he joined them, sliding all the way inside her silken sheath.

When he was buried deep inside her, he released the pent up breath he'd been holding without realizing it. Her hips moved involuntarily and he stilled them instantly. There was no way in hell that he would last if he didn't have a moment to regain his control.

Slowly, as soon as he could manage to do so, he began moving within her. Her body reacted as he knew it would and she began moving with him. Her soft sounds of passion and desire spurred him on and his strokes became deeper and faster. He could tell she was so close to that elusive pinnacle and reached between them to touch her where he knew it would send her over.

It did and the feel of her body tightening around him sent him over the edge with her. He grabbed her hips and held on tight as they both imploded on each other becoming one being for just an instant. The sounds of their pleasure became one as well, echoing off the walls as they held onto each other for dear life.

A few hours later, the mood was far from the way it had been in the sweet moments after their lovemaking. Tired, hot and hungry, their tempers began to fray and they snapped at each other more often than not. When Elizabeth lost her footing and slipped, Jake yelled at her. He knew it was unintentional and was immediately remorseful but it was too late and her green eyes shot daggers that would have killed a lesser man.

"Fine," she bit out. "You do it."

She turned and stomped away, knowing it was childish but not really caring. Logically, she knew that he hadn't meant to yell at her or to hurt her feelings. It was just a reaction. Still she refused to turn around and go back until, about three steps later, Jake seized her arm.

He turned her toward him and sighed. His arms closed around her in a warm hug as he muttered an apology against the top of her head. Her body remained stiff against him for a moment before she relented and returned the hug.

They agreed that perhaps it was time for a break. Each grabbed one end of the couch they had been removing from the almost empty apartment and carefully carried it down the stairs. Once it was safely in the back of the moving truck, Jake closed and latched the door, securing all his belongings inside.

While he saw to that, Elizabeth climbed the

stairs once more to make sure the door to the apartment was closed and locked. They would take this load over to the new place then grab a late lunch, they had decided. She rejoined him moments later, handing over his keys before climbing into the passenger's side of the van.

Later that night, the pair laughed as they sat on the sofa in Jake's new apartment. Most of his belongings were still packed away so they had ordered pizza and grabbed plates, glasses and napkins from Elizabeth's place. They had toyed briefly with the idea of eating at her place since she had a TV and cable already set up. The fact that they usually ended up talking through the shows anyway determined that they would dine in his living room instead.

Elizabeth looked around and hid a grimace. She knew that, in a few days, the place would look much better. After he'd had some time to get settled and unpacked, there would be art on the walls, pictures of his family, knick-knacks his mother had given him over the years. For now though, the plain white walls seemed cold, blank and boring to her. The only saving grace was the man sitting only a few inches away from her.

As she took another bite of pizza, she continued looking around the room they occupied. To be completely honest, it wasn't much different from her own living room and she had been there for years. She had no family pictures. She hadn't ever bothered to find any paintings or other décor for the apartment.

There just didn't seem to be a point with it being just her. It wasn't like she cared that much about it. If that was the case though, a small voice in her mind taunted, why did it bother her so much that Jake's apartment looked the same at the moment?

She tried to silence the voice with the reason that it was very unlike Jake. Jake was anything but cold and boring. He was vibrant and sexy and energetic.

And, at the moment, he was staring at her trying to get her attention. She laughed, realizing she had been a million miles away. Jake must have said something she didn't hear and been waiting for a response.

"Sorry," she grinned sheepishly.

"No worries," he answered lightly. "Though I was about to call NASA and have them go on a search and rescue mission."

She made a face at his teasing and threw her wadded up napkin at him. Suddenly, she was incredibly exhausted. Good thing her apartment was only next door. Otherwise, she might not make it.

A yawn escaped and she stretched sleepily as he watched, smiling. Her shirt rose and revealed a narrow strip of skin across her belly. The smooth, warm flesh there teased him with the memory of how it had felt earlier that day.

Damn, she was going to be the death of him, he realized. One time with her and he couldn't stop thinking about doing it again. And again. And again. Ok so twice, but still.

He had the feeling that he could be with her every single night for the rest of his life and it would never be enough. He wished things wouldn't be so complicated for them, that their friendship didn't stand in the way of the other things he wanted to badly to explore with her.

Absently, he reached over and wrapped a curl of dark red silk around his finger, tugging lightly as her eyes went to his face. Not for the first time, and certainly not the last, he allowed himself to *briefly* imagine that this was their real life. He could so easily picture them together, husband and wife, raising children together, falling asleep in each other's arms, making love each night.

Somewhere deep inside, he also suspected that he was already madly in love with her. He refused to acknowledge it and would never admit it for anything, but he knew it was at least a possibility. If he wasn't so afraid of losing his best friend and hurting her, he might be willing to risk it. The truth was though, that he couldn't imagine his life without Elizabeth in it. When he tried, his chest clenched and refused to allow him to breathe, his heart would pound painfully in his ribs and his throat swelled shut so tightly he couldn't even swallow.

Abruptly, he released the hair he'd been toying with and, grabbing both Elizabeth's plate and his own, he rose to dispose of the trash. A brief look of bewilderment passed across her face at the sudden shift in his disposition, but she said nothing. In a way, he wished she would ask and was pained that she didn't. Yet he was also grateful she hadn't mentioned anything.

He re-entered the room a couple minutes later and found her still in the same spot on the couch. She was staring off into space at absolutely nothing. Lord only knew what she was thinking. Her eyes were dry but glassy and he knew she was somewhere far away. He laughed bitterly at himself inside, thinking she was probably cursing his name for the way he'd been acting today.

First, he made love to her, then yelled at her. Then, a while later he was playing with her hair and then jumped up like he'd been burned. He would be a little confused too, he admitted reluctantly.

Softly, he murmured her name, hoping to draw her from her reverie without startling her. Her eyes remained glazed for a moment before refocusing on him and darting away almost guiltily. Perhaps he'd been right after all about the trail her thoughts had been following.

"You look tired," he almost whispered.

She merely nodded a little, not sure what to say. Another yawn broke through and she tried to smother it but failed. Her eyes were the color of the evergreens outside their building and he knew her well enough to know that it meant she was absolutely exhausted. He loved the color but hated that she was so tired. He hated even more that it was probably his fault.

"You should probably-"

"I should probably-"

They both broke off chuckling awkwardly and yet neither of them moved. Jake looked out the window at the darkened sky. If he was still across town, he would just have her stay with him. Did the fact that they were next door to each other now somehow make that unacceptable? Or did the knowledge that they had made love so hotly earlier and that he wanted to do it again make it unallowable?

"You know," he began, "I know you're just right next door, but maybe…"

Even as the words left his mouth, he called himself a glutton for punishment. Why else would he have even *considered* asking her to stay? Was he insane? Yeah, probably.

She cocked her head to the side almost afraid to wonder if he was saying what she thought he was. A single eyebrow asked the question she dared not. She really hated being so self-conscious sometimes. So many times, she could not bring herself to say or ask what was on her mind.

He shrugged, this time being the one who was uneasy. That was a change for him. Even though he was always slightly off kilter around her, he was never this bad.

"Maybe you could stay here tonight anyway?" he asked finally.

The widening of her eyes and the shock evident on her face told him he had surprised her by actually voicing the question. She didn't seem upset, just taken aback. He'd give anything to know what thoughts were going through her pretty head at that moment. Was she scared, angry, happy?

Suddenly a smile brightened her face and she nodded.

"I'd like that."

"You would?" he couldn't keep the surprise from his voice when he spoke.

"Yeah," she agreed somewhat shyly. "But what will you do for blankets? All yours are still packed away and all the stuff I had at your old place is still somewhere in one of these boxes."

He shrugged. It wasn't that cold in the living room. Anytime they spent the night, he always took the couch and it didn't matter if it was his place or hers. This time would be no different, he chided himself sternly.

He was not about to allow himself to sleep in the same bed with her again. His sanity couldn't take it this time. Between torturing himself with sleeping beside her and trying not to touch her, or sleeping on the couch and being uncomfortable, he'd take the latter. He'd been a glutton for punishment where she was concerned for years.

It only took a few minutes of digging through a couple of the boxes to locate one of Jake's T-shirts. The garment came almost to her knees so she didn't need the sweats he offered to try to find for her. They had set up the bed in his room and she turned back the sheets before disappearing into the bathroom.

A quick shower before she slipped on the T-shirt went a long way toward relaxing her tired muscles and she was more ready than before to crawl between the sheets on the bed. Minutes later, she was sound asleep.

# Chapter 8

She was having that dream again. Her mind knew it but she was helpless, as always, to stop it. She was alone in her room and her sheets were soaked. The dream was always the same. It inevitably woke her, shaking and crying, from even the deepest sleep.

A foreign sound woke Jake from a deep sleep. It wasn't anything loud. It was barely audible. He forced his gritty eyes open and sat up on the couch. Dragging a hand down his face, he reached for his phone. Flinching against the sudden brightness, he forced his eyes to focus on the digits showing on the screen. Just before two a.m. What had awakened him?

Another soft sound caught his ear and he frowned. It had come from his room. Elizabeth was restless sometimes and he wondered if she had woken again with one of her frequent nightmares. She would have awful nightmares, wake up in a cold sweat and be unable to get back to sleep for hours. Sometimes, she would just pace and bite her nails till the sun came up. Other times, she would start cleaning. Still others, she would just lie there silently weeping for whatever she'd dreamt.

He had asked her about it once, suspecting that the cause was something to do with the loss of her parents. She had been unusually close-mouthed about it though, simply denying that it was anything to do with her parents at all. When he'd pressed the issue, asking what it was that bothered her so, she'd clammed up.

That had been one of the rare fights they'd had. He'd been hurt and upset that she was shutting him out of her pain, refusing to let him help. She'd been defensive and upset that he was pushing her so hard to share something she obviously wasn't able to talk about.

The bedroom door was slightly open and he could see that indeed the bedside lamp was on. All the blankets were tossed aside as if the bed's occupant had grown too hot for their comfort. There was no body under them though, he realized as he slowly entered the room. His eyes scanned the area and narrowed when he didn't see Elizabeth anywhere.

A loud clap of thunder sounded right outside the apartment and he realized that the door leading from his room to the balcony was open just a crack. Had she gone outside in this storm, he wondered. Quickly and silently, he crossed the room to the glass that separated him from the outside world.

The vision that greeted his eyes took his breath away and froze him solid. Elizabeth, still in the T-shirt he'd given her to wear to bed, stood in the pouring rain. Her face was turned up to the heavens, the cold water streaming through the sodden tresses of her hair. Rain rolled off her cheeks and coursed down her neck before getting lost in the soaked fabric adorning her otherwise naked body.

Her arms were outstretched as if she were going to hug the storm to her. Another flash of lightening illuminated the rain soaked woman in front of him and he noticed that her lips were parted just slightly, catching the drops as they landed there. As he stared, he watched her body shudder and he realized she was crying again.

He had only seen her do this once before and she had been upset then too. Suddenly, he was torn between going to her and offering her the comfort he knew only he could give or leaving the room and giving her the privacy she no doubt wanted. Then, the decision was taken from him. Lightning split the sky once more and at once the dark green eyes were focused on him.

The impact of the raw emotion in her gaze hit

him like a kick in the gut. So many feelings deep in those eyes. She moved toward him and he remained rooted to the spot.

When she neared the door, he slid it open to allow her entry back into the room. Water continued to pour off of her body and he watched as her nipples reacted to the cooler air in the apartment, tightening to hard pink points under the translucent material. She didn't speak when she reached him. There was no need.

Without a word he reached past her to close the door and pulled the vertical blinds shut as well. Her arms raised over her head much as they had earlier in the day and he stripped the sopping garment from her tossing it carelessly aside. He stooped slightly to scoop her up in his arms.

Seconds later, he laid her perfect, naked form on the bed, following her descent to the mattress. His lips touched hers, this time the spark set off an explosion of immense proportions. Control was a foreign concept to him; restraint, unheard of.

All the years of fighting his attraction to her were history. Every single time he'd turned away from her to protect them both and maintain the distance he thought they needed, were in vain. He was helpless to resist her this time. Even though he knew he would hate himself and regret it in the morning, he knew he was lost.

Within seconds, he too was bare from head to toe. Their bodies fit together perfectly, as if they had been made for each other and he slid against her, warming her icy skin with his own. He felt as if he were on fire as the delicious coolness of her slowly penetrated his being.

His mouth covered one taut pink peak, making her gasp his name in delight. It seemed as if his hands were everywhere, touching and caressing her whole body at once. It was so much more than she could stand, and yet not nearly enough.

Then, he was inside her. This time their joining was hard and fast. There was no gentleness or tenderness, only deep aching need. All Elizabeth saw in his eyes as she gazed up at him, was a hunger and fire that matched the intensity of the storm outside.

His swift, sure strokes quickly lifted her to the highest peaks of ecstasy and he swallowed his name as it left her lips. Her body tightened around him and he gritted his teeth against the urge to fill her then and there. Fingers sliding hesitantly over his skin blew that plan out of the water and he yelled her name as his being emptied into her.

Unable to move, he remained poised over her for a few moments. Damn, he thought to himself. He had not intended to do this again, certainly not so soon. Twice in less than a day, he'd dropped his guard and done the unthinkable. There was just something about her that got under his skin and made him irrational.

As his heart and breathing slowly returned to normal, he realized their fingers were now laced together on either side of her head. Her breathing was still rough and unsteady and her face pink from the exertion moments before. Carefully, he raised himself over her and lay beside her on the bed.

They both stared at the ceiling for long moments as silence filled the air. Finally, he risked a look in her direction. Though there was no smile, her eyes glowed and he couldn't help hoping that he was the cause of that light.

Rolling onto his side, he raised himself on one elbow as he looked down at her. She realized he was staring and moved to cover herself. His hand grasped her wrist stopping her from obscuring this most perfect view.

Unable to help himself, he grinned a little when she began to squirm uncomfortably under his gaze. She really was quite beautiful, but he knew if he spoke the words aloud, she would deny them. He released her before reclaiming his prior position at her side and slid his arm under her shoulders to pull her close.

Elizabeth tried to bite back a smile as Jake pulled her to him. His hand stroked her back while her slender fingers toyed with the tangle of hair dusting his chest. They remained silent for several long minutes as Elizabeth drifted off, she imagined he apologized to her again.

The next morning, Jake awoke alone but could hear Elizabeth moving around somewhere in the apartment. He dressed and ventured out to find her unpacking items and cooking breakfast for them. It had been a while since she had done that.

"Morning, handsome," she greeted him, smiling.

He grunted, still more asleep than awake, and made his way around the end of the counter into the kitchen where he caught her and wrapped her in a tight hug. She hugged him back and lifted a quick peck on his lips before setting a cup of steaming coffee in front of him on the counter.

"Oh God, I love you," he groaned, taking a long drink of the hot, dark brew.

Elizabeth caught her breath and turned away,

pretending to have not been affected by his words. He was joking and only said it because of the coffee, she knew. Still, to hear those words from him was more than she'd ever imagined. God, if only he meant that.

For now, though, she played it off.

"I'll bet you say that to all the girls who bring you coffee first thing in the morning," she joked.

"Nope, just you," he responded in kind.

"Breakfast is almost ready."

"Thank you. You didn't have to do that," he added.

"I know. I wanted to. Go. Sit," she ordered with false sternness.

Jake shook his head and took another sip of his coffee. Instead of sitting though, he placed the cup on the end table by his sofa and started opening some of the boxes they had left in the living room the night before.

Slowly, things were put away and pictures hung on the wall. As the day progressed, the apartment began to come together and by the end of the day most everything was unpacked and in its place.

Late in the afternoon, there was a knock at the door and Jake's family walked in. The small dwelling was instantly full and loud. Elizabeth stood in the hallway looking over the people who had been the closest thing to a family she'd had in years. These were the people who meant more to her than anyone else alive.

Brad and Laura had brought dessert and it was quickly stowed in the refrigerator. Logan and Nick brought fried chicken, mashed potatoes and gravy, salad, vegetables and biscuits. Jake didn't have a table so everyone kind of crowded into the living room, grabbing seats where they could.

Laura claimed the big, overstuffed armchair that took up one corner, while Brad perched himself on the arm at her side. Nick and Logan each staked out prime spots on the floor that allowed them to use Jake's coffee table as a dining table. Jake and Elizabeth ended up next to each other on the couch.

Even while everyone was eating, there was rarely a pause in the conversation. The boys were apologizing that they hadn't been able to make it the previous day to help with moving things. Elizabeth and Jake exchanged a private look knowing that things would have gone much differently had his brothers been able to assist with the move after all.

Laura asked Elizabeth how business was and Elizabeth was thrilled to tell her business was booming. She was actually considering hiring yet another therapist due to the number of people she was having to turn away due to lack of availability. The events of the previous day were relegated to the back of Jake and Elizabeth's minds as the conversations flowed around them.

It was several hours before the two of them were alone again, and by then Jake's apartment looked far more like a home. Pictures had been hung and furniture arranged into its appropriate places.

Katie and the kids had come over after the baby woke up from her nap. Evie had been passed around among the adults, each taking their turn coddling the infant. Even Elizabeth had cuddled the baby for a short time and Jake couldn't help thinking how good she looked with the child in her arms. Her face had turned scarlet when the baby decided she was hungry and began rooting against Elizabeth's breast. She had quickly handed Evie back to her mother to perform the task she could not.

The good-natured laughter continued through the rest of the day. As the hour grew later though, the group began to head to their respective homes. Brad and Laura were the last to leave.

Jake hugged and kissed his mother goodbye

and closed the door behind her. Elizabeth was in the kitchen finishing the cleanup from dinner. He joined her in the small space, just leaning his hip against the counter as he watched her.

His almost empty glass of soda sat near him and he picked it up. He wanted to reach for her and the glass occupied his hands so he wouldn't. Instead, he took small sips as she completed her tasks.

Something tugged at him deep inside as his eyes lingered on her. He frowned as the realization hit him. All his efforts these past years had been for nothing. Every bit of self-control he'd forced himself to exert was wasted. Now his heart was telling him that he had done what he'd feared for so long. He had fallen in love with Elizabeth.

The room spun crazily as his chest tightened. If he didn't know better, he'd swear he'd just been caught off guard by a sucker punch. He needed to get out of here. Now. God help him, what had he done?

Elizabeth looked up at him from the sink where she was just finishing up. Concern tightened her features as she pinned him with a searching look. Something was wrong. She could feel it. He looked positively dumbfounded.

"Hey, you ok?"

"Yeah," he lied tightly, "I just have to…um…I'm really tired and forgot I'm picking up an extra shift tomorrow."

Something flashed briefly within her eyes and he knew she could tell he was lying. He braced himself, expecting an argument, or at the very least for her to call him out on it. Instead, she nodded once and pushed past him. Within seconds, she had grabbed her things and disappeared through his door.

Seconds later, he heard her own apartment door slam with far more force than was necessary. Damn, he hadn't wanted to upset her, but he had to get some time away to clear his head. He had to figure out what to do in light of this new realization.

The apartment felt barren and empty in the wake of her departure and Jake swore. She hadn't even said goodbye. Nor had she hugged him. In fact, she hadn't said a word. He swore again, this time sending his glass crashing against the wall on the other side of the room. The dish shattered, leaving a mess that did nothing at all to improve his mood.

Dammit all to hell, he thought. He had no idea what to do now. For years, he'd fought against this very thing. He'd been afraid of ruining their friendship, afraid of hurting her, or himself.

Now, he realized it had been for nothing.

With a dismayed sigh, he snatched his keys from the counter and stalked to the front door. He wasn't going to sleep tonight, he knew. Maybe a few hours at the gym would help clear his head enough to figure out what the hell to do.

Minutes later, Jake stood in front of one of the full length mirrors at the gym. His muscles rippled as he lifted the dumbbells with alternating arms, but the exercise failed to numb his mind and heart. God, he had no idea what to do. He was scared to death.

This was Elizabeth for crying out loud. It was one thing to screw up with someone else. If he messed up with her though...God, he couldn't lose Elizabeth. But he knew he would. Inevitably he would screw up. He always did.

But, whispered a small voice, he'd screwed up before with her. She hadn't left. She had told him once that she loved him. He wondered if she still did. Was it too late?

Maybe, just maybe, they actually *could* take a chance. Was it possible that they could actually make it? God, it was so tempting.

Silently, he swore. This wasn't getting him anywhere. He couldn't run anymore. He had run for years only to find he'd gotten nowhere.

Even worse, he'd utterly failed at avoiding the one thing he'd been running from in the first place.

What if all of this was a moot point? What if she didn't want him anymore? What if she never had?

Swearing internally, he dropped the weight. He couldn't do anything else. It was time to lay it on the line.

Elizabeth sighed as she stepped out of the shower. As soon as she had left Jake's, she'd gone for a run. That had been well over an hour ago. She'd needed to clear her head.

It hadn't worked. She still had no idea what the hell was going on. All she knew was that she loved him as much as she ever had. At this point, she was reasonably sure that there was no force in heaven or on earth that was going to change that.

She also knew he did *not* love her. He had made that so very clear. No force on heaven or earth would ever change that either. She had tried so hard, so many times, to move on. It hadn't worked. It never did. So where did that leave her?

It took her almost a full minute to realize that someone was pounding on her door. She'd heard it dimly in her reverie, and wondered how long it had been going on before she fully realized. Hurriedly, she wrapped the towel around herself and ran down the hallway.

Another knock elicited an exasperated promise of "I'm coming!" She looked through the small peephole in the door to see Jake on the other side. Nothing could have surprised her more.

Elizabeth threw open the door and Jake rushed in, closing it behind him. There was an almost wild look in his eyes and Elizabeth felt her heart skip a beat. Had something happened? Why was he back?

"You shouldn't have answered the door like that," he admonished, noticing the towel precariously held in place over her breasts. The bottom edge, barely covered her backside and it was all he could do to not stare.

"I knew it was you," she retorted, still unsure as to what he was doing here.

"Why-" she began.

"I need to talk to you. I couldn't wait. I'm sorry. I know it's late. I had to…I don't know I had to get out. I was trying to think. It didn't help."

Elizabeth frowned, wondering what in the world could possibly have this normally easy-going man so worked up. If she didn't know any better, she would actually think he was nervous. It kind of made *her* nervous and she wondered if whatever was coming was a conversation that should be had in a bath towel.

"I've been thinking. Things are different than they used to be between us, Elizabeth. They used to be so easy and that's changed now."

Elizabeth swallowed against the tightness in her chest. She wasn't sure she liked where this was going. It sounded scarily like he was going to give her the kiss off. God, what was she going to do?

She dropped into the chair behind her, looking up at her friend and hoping she was wrong. Something was definitely bothering him. It was getting so hard to breathe. He couldn't leave her now could he?

"What if we gave it a go?" he asked suddenly.

Elizabeth stared at him blankly, certain that she had suddenly taken a slip down the rabbit hole. Jake was asking her to "give it a go." Give what a go?

"Us," Jake answered her unspoken question.

Elizabeth blinked hard and shook her head, completely and totally lost. She had to have missed something somewhere. What the hell was going on?

"We've been best friends forever, right? And

we know we have chemistry. Why couldn't we put it together and see what we have? Maybe it's enough to make it. I'm not saying there's any guarantee about anything. But what if we could make it? I mean, I can't think of anyone else I'd rather try with now. You've proven you're not going anywhere. Hopefully I've convinced you of the same. Why can't we see if we have what it takes?"

"Wait," Elizabeth interrupted hesitantly and still very confused, "Are you asking me to be your girlfriend? Like to date you?"

The incredulity in her voice almost changed his mind, but he knew he had to at least try. Silently, he nodded. There it was. It was out in the open now and was all up to Elizabeth. If she said no, he'd know. But if she said yes...

"Are you serious? I mean..." she paused for a moment. "You've always...I mean *we've* always...I mean..."

She stopped, unsure what to say now. Never in a million years would she have guessed that Jake would be asking this. Elizabeth searched his eyes for any sign that she was misunderstanding or that this was some kind of a joke or dream. It was everything she had wanted for so long. She was almost afraid to believe.

Still, as she stared, there was nothing to tell

her he was not serious. His gaze still rested on her intently and he had not spoken. He hadn't even moved. If she didn't know better, she would even think he was holding his breath.

She could almost hear him saying "well?" even though she knew he hadn't spoken.

He finally did speak though, his voice hesitant and unsure. It was the only time in her memory that she could recall Jake being unsure of anything.

"It's not like much would change you know?" he offered. "We pretty much spend all our time together now anyway. It would just be, I guess, official. We wouldn't have to try to date anyone else. I wouldn't have to pretend every time I saw you that I didn't want to just take you in my arms and kiss you senseless."

Elizabeth felt the heat rushing to her face at his words. Did he really feel that way? His eyes told her he was being completely sincere and honest.

What could she say? He was offering her everything she had ever wanted. How could she possibly say anything other than of course?

Just to be sure, Elizabeth repeated it once more. She had to be certain. She couldn't stand the thought of being a fool for him again.

"You want me to be your girlfriend, Jake? Is

that what you are asking?"

He nodded, wondering if he'd made a huge mistake in asking her. What if he'd screwed up already just by doing so? Was she angry?

He waited in silence, his gaze trained on her features. For once, he truly had no idea what she was thinking or feeling. That only made the situation more unnerving for him. Jake was used to always being able to tell what was on her mind just by a look at her face. This time, it was no help.

Elizabeth stared back at Jake, just as silent as he was. His own face was inscrutable, hiding all emotion and leaving her at a loss. A hint of anxiety showed for a split second as Jake began to doubt himself, and she knew this was real. A slow smile spread across her face as it finally sank in. He was serious. All she could do was smile even bigger and nod slowly.

"Okay. Yes."

Jake looked stunned. As if he were unable to believe she'd actually agreed to his insane idea. Then he let out a breath he hadn't realized he'd been holding and a smile, scooping her out of the chair and into his arms.

His fingers tangled in her damp hair and angled her head slightly for a deep searching kiss and the towel that had been wrapped around her fell forgotten to the floor between them.

# Chapter 9

The next day, Jake insisted on going to his parents' house and telling them the news. He knew they would be thrilled. Elizabeth wasn't as sure but he was so excited and insistent that she agreed.

His mother teared up and squeezed Elizabeth until she thought she would pass out from lack of oxygen. His father clapped him on the back and congratulated him, giving Elizabeth a hearty hug and a kiss on the cheek. Nick rolled his eyes and told him it was about time and Logan agreed.

It was agreed that they should all celebrate what everyone else apparently believed had been so long in the making. So everyone piled into their respective cars and the entire family invaded the nearest pancake house for a jubilant brunch. Alone in the car with Jake, Elizabeth admitted she'd been slightly nervous about his family's reaction to their new relationship.

"But why? You know they love you. We always have," he told her.

"I know," she shrugged. "I just wasn't sure

how they'd feel about us - you know - actually being together."

Jake smiled and reached over to lace his fingers through hers. "Well do you feel better about it now?"

Elizabeth smiled and nodded. The rest of the day continued on the same note, relaxed but enjoyable. She truly was relieved. Even though she wasn't quite sure what she'd been afraid of, she hadn't anticipated the complete and unconditional acceptance of her new status as Jake's girlfriend.

Nothing really changed to the casual observer. They still spent the weekends at his family's home when they weren't working. The only new thing was the way Jake treated her. It almost seemed like a dream at times.

He no longer kept his distance, physically or emotionally. There was no hesitation about kissing and touching her, either in private or around his family. They went out a lot more, too. Dinner, movies, wherever they felt like going, they'd go. They spent the nights together a lot more often too.

He was a lot less restrained in his lovemaking now and Elizabeth, in turn, felt free to explore a little more. She learned what he liked and what he didn't. It thrilled her to learn what drove him mad and could make that precious control of his snap.

Jake even surprised her with flowers at her office one day. She'd never been much for roses, so Jake had found lovely blue irises and put them in a vase. He'd waited in the lobby, chatting with Katie, until Elizabeth came out. When she'd appeared through the narrow doorway, he'd greeted her with a sweet lingering kiss and handed her the flowers.

Elizabeth had been touched beyond words. No man had ever given her flowers before. For that matter, no one had done a lot of the things Jake did, she thought, blushing at the mere thought. But he continued to surprise her in both little and big ways. Each day seemed a little better than the last.

Only the knowledge of her secret marred the sweetness for Elizabeth as the time went on. Eventually, she knew, she would have to tell Jake what had happened those long years before. She should have told him when it happened and not a day went by that she didn't regret it. The more time passed, the harder it seemed.

Every time the thought pressed in on her, she forced it away. Just one more day, she would promise herself each time. One more day to relish their newfound closeness. One more day to laugh with him and love him without him knowing. Then she would come clean. She would tell him everything. Just one more day.

The weather turned colder as winter approached and things grew busy for both Jake and Elizabeth. Winter was always busier for the fire department with fireplace accidents and Christmas tree fires. And the approaching holidays usually encouraged people to de-stress with a massage. Still, they managed to find time to spend together.

Thanksgiving dawned bright but cold as Jake and Elizabeth drove over to his parents' house. Everybody was going to be there today. Nick, Katie and their kids were coming over later in the afternoon, to allow time for the kids to have naps. Even Logan was going to be there and there had been whispers that he was going to bring a guest, but nobody knew for sure. Elizabeth had her suspicions but had kept them to herself.

Lexi was researching how massage could help sufferers of PTSD, which had gravely affected Logan since his most recent deployment. He had agreed to do an article on Lexi's work, not realizing she was the same woman he'd met in a bar on the other side of the state several months before. Neither of them had ever dreamed that the chance meeting would change their lives.

Despite the fact that they apparently couldn't get along for more than five minutes at a time, Logan made a point of coming in at least once a month for his massage. Lately though, she had noticed a shift in their interactions with each other. While she wouldn't exactly say they had become friends, there was definitely something different. It wouldn't surprise her at all to find out sometime soon that the two were a couple.

The small living room in Brad and Laura's house was already crowded when they arrived. Nick and Katie had ended up coming over earlier than intended after all and a few of the neighbors who'd been invited were already occupying a few of the seats, as well. Laura greeted them both with a hug and a kiss, ushering them inside to mingle with the other guests who'd already been inside.

Elizabeth made her way to the cozy, yet still somehow spacious kitchen. This was what a home should be like, she thought for at least the thousandth time. There were pictures everywhere, even in the kitchen. There was a warmth, an organized chaos that made her feel this was where she belonged.

All these years later, the holidays were still

difficult for her. She still missed her parents terribly and, while Laura and Brad had pretty much made her an integral part of their own family, there were still times that she longed for her own parents to be back. She felt a hand at her back and blinked quickly to banish the moisture that had been welling in her eyes, unnoticed.

Turning, she saw that Jake was behind her. Always far more observant than she would like, he had noticed her hesitation and accurately guessed the reason for it. She swore that man knew her better than anyone on the planet. There was absolutely nothing she could keep from him, save one.

Softly, so that only she could hear, he whispered a concerned, "Are you okay?"

Elizabeth forced a smile and nodded. Jake didn't believe her and told her so. She shrugged and sighed deeply. They'd gone over it a hundred times. They both knew what was bothering her and they both knew there was nothing that could be done about it. She just needed a few minutes and she'd be fine, she promised.

Jake searched her face for another moment. Finally, deciding there was nothing more to be said or done, he nodded tightly. He squeezed her gently and dropped a light kiss on her mouth before walking with her into the kitchen to see what could be done to help.

The rest of the day was spent in a hectic peace. There was no real stress, just a lot to be done and everyone was helping. It was part of what Elizabeth loved about being a part of this family. Once you walked through the front door, you were treated as if you'd always belonged there.

Though it took time, dinner was eventually finished, and the table set. Logan arrived, with Lexi in tow, much as Elizabeth had suspected. The slightly older woman had colored slightly at Elizabeth's knowing look. Although she didn't pry, it was clear to Elizabeth that she'd been right in her prediction.

Finally, everyone was seated and ready to enjoy the delicious looking meal that had been laid out before them. The table fairly groaned under the weight of its burden, but its complaints were drowned out by the cheerful conversations taking place around it. Mashed potatoes, turkey, ham, three kinds of gravy, endless dishes of vegetables and dinner rolls were just a small part of the feast that had been prepared and the smells mingled together in a tantalizing symphony that had everyone's mouth watering.

Brad cleared his throat authoritatively, signaling a pause in the conversation. Once the noise had abated, except for Evie's soft gurgling, everyone joined hands waiting for the Thanksgiving prayer. Although the family was not overly religious, there were still some traditions that were strongly held and the Thanksgiving prayer was one of them.

It was several hours later before people finally began to trickle out of the house. The leftovers had been divided amongst the attendees and most left with the promise of returning the next day for the Christmas tree decorating. That was another favorite tradition of Elizabeth's.

As had been their custom for as long as she had been with them, the Carpenters always put their tree in the day after Thanksgiving. It was always a big to-do and everyone always had a blast. The entire house would get decorated in one day, including the outside lights. There was food, drinks, Christmas carols and an overwhelming feeling of gaiety that generally prevailed throughout the upcoming season anyway.

Wreaths were hung on the door and garland on the mantle. There were battery operated candles in each window, and a nativity scene on the coffee table in the living room. Even mistletoe made an appearance, hanging just inside the front door of the home.

As was tradition for them, Brad and Laura met under the small green sprig for a sweet holiday kiss. Nick and Katie took a turn as well, giving each other as much of a smooch as baby Evie would allow. Her squealed protest at being sandwiched between her parents cut short any show of affection they would have otherwise indulged in.

It was at the party that Jake made the suggestion of going on a day trip for shopping. Elizabeth agreed eagerly. Maybe it would help her figure out what to get him this year. She always had a hard time figuring out what to get him, but this year it seemed even more challenging.

Their new relationship created a new definition of what was appropriate and what was not. The friendly gifts of the past somehow didn't seem suitable. Somehow though, she didn't think more intimate gifts would fit exactly right either.

She still had to tell him of her secret. Perhaps she should tell him while they were out and hope to God that he would accept and forgive what she had to say. She only wished she knew how to start.

It was late when Elizabeth and Jake finally left the festivities to head home. As they said their goodbyes, Laura pointed out, much to Elizabeth's chagrin, that the pair was under the mistletoe. The evil glint in Jake's eyes was the only warning given before he swooped in for a breathtaking kiss that left Elizabeth both aching for him, and coloring with embarrassment. Wolf whistles and catcalls accompanied applause at their first "official" holiday kiss.

Trying to catch her breath, she clung to Jake's arm as they finished their goodbyes. They wanted to get a somewhat early start on their shopping the next day, though that was questionable given that it was already so late. Jake knew that Elizabeth was one of those people who absolutely had to have her eight hours of sleep, or she was a bear to be around. He'd teased her about it occasionally, calling her lazy bones. But Elizabeth was okay with that. She knew she could get testy if she was too tired but allowed that he could get testy at times too, so if she could deal with him when he was being cranky then he could damn well do the same.

After all the cleaning and decorating they had done that day, they both felt a bit sweaty and gritty on top of being worn out. Neither of them felt they would sleep well as they were so it was decided that showers were a must before bed. They agreed that Jake would shower first and then Elizabeth would have her turn, although Jake had teasingly suggested that they could shower together. Elizabeth had grinned and given him a long sexy kiss before pointing out that, while she had no problem whatsoever with the idea, that would almost certainly guarantee a much longer wait before they went to sleep and therefore mean a later start the next morning.

Elizabeth waited in the bedroom while Jake washed himself. Despite her earlier point about not wanting them to be up too late, she found it increasingly tempting to join him in the bathroom. The thought of their slick, soapy bodies mingling in the streams of hot water, their mouths dancing to a song only they knew, was enough to have her thinking that perhaps, instead of a hot shower, hers should be cold. Lord knew it wouldn't be the first time she'd taken a cold shower because of Jake.

As she waited, her mind wandered. Good Lord, that man was taking forever. She wished he would hurry up because she didn't like the track her mind was taking. In spite of itself, her brain seemed determined to keep front and center the thought that she needed to come clean with Jake, both about her feelings and her secret.

Pacing, she paused for a moment at the glass door that led out to the balcony. It was far too cold to go out there tonight, but she almost wished it was raining and that she could. Somehow it calmed her spirit to feel like she was a part of a storm. She'd never quite understood it, just taken the relief when she could.

Suddenly, she felt Jake's arms come around her from behind and jumped. She'd never heard him come out. Quickly, she pasted a smile on her face and turned to hug him. She was determined to enjoy this one last night. Tomorrow was it. It would be the end.

Just for a moment, she stood frozen in front of him, wanting to remember everything as it was right then. The warmth and happiness deep in his beautiful eyes, the softness of his hand against her face, everything that made this as perfect a moment as had ever existed. She knew it would be the last one like this.

Finally, Elizabeth forced herself to move. If she didn't go now, she wouldn't. She would stay right there forever and never face the reality of what was to come.

Jake frowned slightly as Elizabeth disappeared into the room he'd just vacated. There was something different about her tonight. She seemed almost sad. He had no clue why he felt that. It wasn't as if she'd said or done anything to make him think that way. Just, something felt...off.

He shook his head slightly, telling himself he was imagining things. Elizabeth was so easy to read, he'd be able to tell for sure if something was going on. Still, a nagging voice in his head refused to let it rest. With a self-disgusted sigh, he reached for the book he'd left on the nightstand and lay back to read while he waited for Elizabeth to return.

Elizabeth took extra care, brushing her hair a little extra, applying just a touch of sheer gloss to her lips. She wanted everything to be just right. This was going to be the last night she had with Jake, she knew, and wanted everything to be perfect.

Finally, she took a deep breath and opened the door. She stopped short. Jake was there on her bed, fast asleep. The book he'd been reading, lay open on his chest, very lightly held by his fingers.

Inexplicably, she felt a painful lump in her throat as she watched him sleep. At the moment, he looked so peaceful and relaxed. It was a far cry, she knew, from the actual truth. Jake had seen so much, done so much, experienced so much that she knew he never truly was at peace.

As much as she wished she could, it wasn't even anything she could give him. And after tomorrow, she wouldn't even be able to try. She brushed the thought aside one last time as she drank in the sight of him.

This man was everything to her. And tonight was the last night he would be there. She knew there would never again be anyone in her life like Jake. He was her best friend, her lover, her knight in shining armor.

While he never complained, and she knew he would never give up the job, she also had seen the shadows in his eyes. He did his best to keep them hidden, but she could see it sometimes when he let his guard down. Sometimes, he just couldn't help.

Yet, even with that knowledge, he went in day after day, call after call. Whenever he was needed, he went gladly, without a thought for his own safety. This man who was sleeping before her now, was the definition of a hero.

At last, Elizabeth padded silently over to the bed, climbing on carefully so as not to wake him. She ached to touch him, but not yet. With more tenderness than she'd ever known it was possible to feel she whispered softly, "I love you, Jacob Alexander Carpenter. Please always remember that."

Then she leaned over and ever so gently pressed her lips to his. Jake's eyes drifted open lazily as he came awake and responded to the soft caress of her mouth. The freshly showered scent of her stirred his nether regions almost as much as the long, lingering kiss she was bestowing on him.

When at last she raised her head, Jake was fairly certain that he had never been kissed like that in his entire life. Not even by her. That was only the beginning.

Determined that, whatever the outcome of the next day, they would never forget this one night, Elizabeth put all she had learned about him to work that night. She kissed and touched every inch of skin, using her hands and mouth to slowly but surely drive him out of his mind.

A hot, moist trail of kisses over his jaw led down the side of his neck to his collarbone. Her fingers preceded her mouth as it made its way down his rapidly heating body. Barely making contact with his skin, she dragged her hands gently over his chest and down his belly, followed closely by her lips. He groaned aloud when her hair swept across his hardness.

She kissed and touched all around it, making the area so sensitive he didn't think he could take any more. The warmth of her breath on him almost undid him before she backed off again. Finally, she dropped a sweet, gentle kiss on the most sensitive part of his body before at last taking him into her mouth. He was certain she was going to kill him with her teasing when she withdrew her mouth and slid up his body.

Just when he thought she was finally going to give him what they both wanted and join them together, she would back off and return to driving him mad. When at last, he could bear no more, he lunged upward with a soft growl.

"No more," he managed through a clenched jaw.

In one motion he sat up, grabbed Elizabeth and rolled her under him. The next second he was fully buried inside the sweet, hot embrace of her femininity. Despite her efforts to deny it, it was clear her teasing had affected her as much as it had him. There was no resistance at all as he slid inside her.

With long, powerful strokes, he pushed them both toward some invisible peak. They both knew where it was but it was known only to them. He was certain no other lovers had ever felt the way they did when they came together. With one final thrust, he called out her name, relishing her answering cry.

When he was able to move again finally, he

rolled off of her to his side, bringing her body with him and tucking her snugly against his ribs. In the dark silence, they held each other as their heartbeats returned to normal and sleep set in. Just as he fell asleep, Jake smiled with the knowledge that this was his forever. Nothing could ever break them apart.

# Chapter 10

They had decided they would go somewhere and have a nice leisurely breakfast before setting out on their trip. A nice cup of coffee to wake them both up, accompanied by bacon, biscuits, waffles and eggs. It was far more than Elizabeth could ever have hoped to finish off in one sitting.

It didn't help that her stomach was in knots of anticipation and anxiety. She knew Jake better than almost anyone, and he her. But that didn't necessarily mean she knew how he would react. She couldn't help but feel slightly panicky every time she thought about what she had to do.

They spent the day ducking in and out of malls and quaint little shops looking for special little items they thought people would enjoy. They laughed at the silly hats in one store as they took turns trying them on. In another store, they found eclectic little items like digital key chains and forks that would tell one whether they were making a good food choice.

After a few hours, Jake suggested that that they take a break and do a little sightseeing. There was an old stone tower nearby that frequently drew tourists and he thought it might be nice to go take a look. It took only minutes to climb to the top and once there, they were able to enjoy the spectacular view. Or at least Jake was.

Elizabeth looked down and instantly regretted it, her head swimming sickeningly. Jake grabbed her elbow to steady her.

"You okay?" he asked, concerned.

She nodded faintly and spoke in little more than a whisper, "Forgot for a moment that I was afraid of heights."

To his credit, only one corner of his mouth turned up. He too had forgotten.

"Come here, I'll keep you safe," he offered.

She hung back for a moment, biting her lip.

"But, what if I'm afraid of you?" she asked.

He looked shocked as he answered, "Why on earth would you be afraid of me?"

She looked away, realizing she had said too much. Oh well, there was no going back now. Her dark blue green eyes met his warm brown ones once more.

"Because I could fall for you as easily as I could fall from here, easier probably. And it would hurt a hell of a lot more."

He stared at her for a moment, his expression unreadable, and she looked away unable to bear the scrutiny anymore. Her cheeks heated with embarrassment. She knew she had said too much. She should have stopped while she was ahead.

"You think you could fall for me?" he asked at last, his voice soft but steady.

Elizabeth's teeth snagged the tender skin of her lip once more and she searched for the words she needed to say to him. There was so much to tell him. She knew he wouldn't want anything to do with her when she was done. It was confession time.

"Let's go outside," she suggested, her chest feeling tight, and he nodded.

The bright sunlight of the late fall day blinded them both as they exited the small tower. Both flinching against the sudden brightness, they made their way over to a bench that lined the walkway. Elizabeth sat and motioned for him to do the same, before standing once more. She couldn't sit still.

"What's up honey?" he asked, softly, a feeling of foreboding knotting his gut.

"I was going to tell you something before…" she broke off, her face coloring again.

He nodded.

"Um, I actually have a couple of confessions to make," she began, wiping her hands down her jeans nervously.

He sat up a little straighter, not sure he wanted to hear what was coming next, whatever it was. She looked upset enough to make him sure he didn't want to know. An abnormally icy breeze came up and he watched as she shivered, huddling down in her coat.

Elizabeth felt the wind cut through her coat as if she were naked. It was positively frigid. Was it a harbinger of the cold to come? Finally, she took a deep breath and began speaking.

"First of all, I lied up there when I said I could fall for you."

Inexplicably, a knife sliced through his chest at her words. Damn, he had *wanted* to believe she could fall for him. He hadn't realized it until recently. Now, though, hearing her say she'd lied about being able to fall for him...unless she meant...

She spoke again, "I already have fallen for you. Hell, I think I fell for you all the way back in high school, Jake. I can't remember when I didn't love you."

She blinked hard and looked away again, shoving her hands into her pockets.

"I tried. God, I tried so hard not to love you. I tried to ignore it, to pretend it wasn't there. I tried to convince myself not to, to convince myself I didn't. Anything and everything I could think of. But I can't change it. When you asked me to be your girlfriend, you gave me everything I've wanted for as long as I can remember. How could I possibly say no?"

A smile split his face, then faded when she looked back at him, unbearable pain and sorrow in her eyes. Whatever was coming next, he definitely didn't want to hear. He started to stand to stop her, but she stepped back away and he merely stood and stayed where he was.

"But now...oh God...I don't even know how to start. I want more but there can't be more yet. Not till you know everything. Do you, um, remember a few months after I graduated, I left for a while?"

He nodded. Of course, he remembered. It was the longest few weeks he could remember. It had been the only time since they'd met that they hadn't seen each other at least once a week.

"I had to go away. I didn't go to look for distant family. The night that we...on my birthday," she couldn't say the words even now and didn't know why.

"I got pregnant."

All the color left Jake's face and she forced herself to continue.

"I know. I couldn't believe it either. Um,

then," she swallowed harder and almost choked. "A couple weeks later, things started happening. Bad things."

He watched as tears rolled, unnoticed down her face. She'd lost the baby. *Their* baby. The baby he hadn't even known existed. He got it now. Searching her face, hoping he was wrong, he backed away.

She had gotten pregnant with his child the night he'd slept with her. Never saying a word, she had gone on pretending everything was ok. Then she'd lost the baby and still never spoken a word to him about it.

His voice was harsh when he spoke and she recoiled.

"You lost the baby."

It was a statement not a question. She nodded and watched as his face paled even more if possible. She could see he was reeling with shock at what she'd told him.

"You never told me. Not a word. You lied to me," he accused.

"I know and I am so sorry, Jake. Really. You have to believe me I never meant to hurt you or anything. That's why –" she broke off at the poisonous glare he shot her.

As cold as ice, he stared at the woman he thought he'd known. The woman who had been his best friend for years. He stared at her now, realizing he'd never known her at all if she could keep something like this from him for so long. The knife that had slashed through him moments before was nothing compared to the pain he felt now.

She reached out to him and he drew away.

"Please, Jake. You have to listen. You have to understand," she pleaded in a whisper.

He turned on her then, the ice gone and replaced by a raging inferno.

"Understand what? That you got pregnant with my child and didn't tell me? That you – that you *lost* my child and didn't tell me?" his voice broke.

"I wanted to –"

"Then you should have. I thought I was your best friend! That you could tell me anything. Jesus, that was *my* baby too, Elizabeth! When the hell were you going to tell me?"

"I don't know! I couldn't! I tried. I went to see you at the station the night I found out. They said you were busy but I didn't realize what they meant by busy till I saw you with Lisa, Linda, Liza whatever the hell her name was. I couldn't tell you when you –"

"Save it! This was eight years ago! Why the hell didn't you tell me before now? Say something, anything, about it? Ever?"

Now she yelled at him, too.

"I couldn't damn it! What was I going to tell you? That the little girl you'd fu-"

"Don't say that word," he warned, flinching as she finished the ugly term for what they'd done.

"That you'd gotten her pregnant? That you weren't even divorced from your wife yet and you were going to have a child by someone you still considered a child?" she carelessly flung at him, the words he'd cut her so deeply with that night. "And that while you were still trying to be the single guy again, having your fun with any girl who'd have you, that I was going to have your baby?"

"You still should have told me," his voice was hard as stone.

"I know that. And believe me I wanted to. I needed you so bad –"

"Obviously, not badly enough to tell me the truth," he bit off.

"Jake, please. I'm telling you this because I wanted you to know. Because I love you."

Instantly he was inches from her face, glowering down at her.

Between his teeth, he swore. "Don't! Don't you dare say that to me. If you did, you'd have told me years ago. So how did you 'lose' this baby anyway? Or did you even lose it really?"

She flinched as if he'd struck her and stood speechless for a moment as the implication of his accusation sunk in.

"You bastard," she spit. "You have no idea what I went through when I lost that child!"

Knowing she was about half a second from losing control completely, she turned away, taking only a couple steps before he grabbed her, pinning her against a nearby tree.

"Oh no, you don't. You're not running away this time. This time we finish it. You ran away earlier. And you ran away years ago. You're not getting away this time."

She said nothing, refusing to meet his eyes. Just a few more moments and it would all be over, she knew. He would leave and everything they had and could be, would be gone.

"I would have known if you'd told me. I would have been there for you."

"Would you, Jake? Think about it. Really? With everything that was going on, would you have been there? No you're right. You would have. You'd have insisted on marrying me because you felt you couldn't leave me alone to raise your baby. When I lost the baby, then what? How long would you have stayed after that?"

He released her, bitter and defeated and raw. The one woman he'd thought could never hurt him, had just dealt him the biggest blow of his life and he wasn't sure he could survive it. Her betrayal hurt far worse than Sharon's ever had.

"I guess you'll never know."

"Jake, wait…"

"Yes, Elizabeth, I would have married you. I would have done the right thing. And I'd have stayed."

"I couldn't chain you down like that. That's part of why I couldn't tell you before I lost it. I couldn't force you into marriage like that. If you'd stayed, you'd have been stuck with someone you didn't want, all because of a 'big stupid mistake' I believe you called it. How could I do that to you?"

"It should have been my choice, damn it! You should have let me make that decision. You had no right to choose *for* me! Did it ever occur to you that maybe I would have *wanted* to marry you? That maybe we could have been happy together? Raised a family? Did you ever think maybe I was a grown man and able to make my own decisions?"

"Oh yeah, that was exactly what I thought after you had made it so crystal clear that you didn't want me, didn't love me and never would!" she retorted.

The small part of him that was still logical and rational told him she had a point. However, the larger, more emotional part of him that was still reeling with the impact of her revelation refused to accept that. There was no excuse.

"It still should have been my decision."

With that, he turned to walk away, leaving her alone as she'd known he would.

Still, she reached after him and called out.

"Jake, please try to understand. I love you."

He paused and looked over his shoulder, the pain in his face tearing her apart even more.

"The hell of it is, Elizabeth, I love you too. Goodbye."

Then he was gone.

The days had turned into weeks and time blurred together for Elizabeth as the holidays approached. Work and home seemed to merge and she couldn't spend more than a couple hours at home without being in bed. Otherwise, she thought. A lot. And hurt. A lot.

She missed Jake so much. He hadn't moved out yet, though she expected him to any day now. A couple of times, she'd seen him in passing but he'd never acknowledged her presence. Not that she was surprised. The only thing that had surprised her was how much it had hurt when he'd told her he loved her as he'd walked away from her.

It killed her, when she did see him, to see the anguish in his eyes and to know that she was the reason for it. Hurting Jake was the last thing she'd ever wanted to do. And she'd done it in spades. Now, she couldn't even be there to help him when he needed someone. Then again, she thought, maybe he didn't.

The moisture on her cheeks brought her back to the present and she realized that the phone on her desk was ringing. It was the director of the nursing home, again. She wanted to finalize the details of the contract they were about to sign. Elizabeth should have been thrilled to get it. She had worked so hard and wouldn't have gotten it without Jake's encouragement and support.

Now, she could tell Katie and Lexi that they had solid full time paychecks coming. They would be overjoyed. She should be too. Instead, she only felt empty.

She hung up the phone and turned to stare out the window. It was snowing again. Mid December in New England, it did that a lot. At least she'd gotten her snow tires on the truck already. One of the few things she had remembered to do since Jake had gone away.

Several times, she had debated cornering him at the station so he couldn't escape and demanding he listen to her, but she knew that wouldn't help. The only thing that would do was cause a scene and she could do without that. She wondered if he had told anyone else about what had happened between them.

The little bell over the front door jingled and one of her favorite clients, Ethel Collins, strolled in. An elderly woman, she made regular visits to Elizabeth and swore it helped her with every ailment she had. Only slightly stooped at seventy-five, she was doing better than most people at her age.

Elizabeth stood and crossed to the older woman and took her arm. The white haired woman was still pretty strong and able to get around on her own. Nonetheless, she was a bit shaky sometimes and Elizabeth always went out of her way to help her.

A few moments later, Elizabeth was lost in the comforting rhythm that had long since become a part of her. It was as natural to her as breathing and it was easy to give herself over to the solace of the familiar process. She was so engrossed that it startled her when Ethel spoke.

"So, how are things going with that young man of yours?"

The question took Elizabeth off guard and her hands faltered as she caught her breath It was one of the many times she was grateful a client couldn't see her response to something they had said.

She and Ethel always chatted amicably while Elizabeth worked on her, and Ethel knew a lot of Elizabeth's history, including her closeness with Jake and her family. Several times, Ethel had hinted she hoped Elizabeth and Jake would end up together. Elizabeth had harbored that same hope, she admitted to herself now. But it was not to be.

As it was now, it was a full minute before Elizabeth was able to force her hands to resume their fluid strokes over the thin skin beneath her fingers. Injecting a light note into her voice, she assured Ethel that Jake was doing just fine. At least she hoped he was. She wouldn't know though to be honest.

"Now honey, you don't think I'm buying that do you?"

Elizabeth feigned innocence and claimed to not know what the older woman was referring to.

"In all the years I've been seeing you, and all the conversations we've had, not once have you been thrown off your stride. Not till now. Tell

Ethel what happened," she insisted.

"It's too much to go into right now, Ethel. Everything will be fine. There's just a lot of stuff going on. Nothing major."

A scoff from the woman on the table let Elizabeth know she was still unconvincing in her denial.

"That boy leave you?" she asked.

"Not really, Ethel. It's kind of complicated. I screwed up."

The woman hmph, "Couldn't have been that bad."

Elizabeth forced herself to make a noncommittal response and quickly changed the subject. She couldn't recall ever being so grateful for a session to end. It hadn't occurred to her that some of the clients who were closer to her would ask about Jake. Nor had she thought about the fact that in their town, some clients were bound to have seen them together in the past few weeks.

She excused herself from the room and went to get a cup of water as she always did, hoping Ethel wouldn't mention Jake again. It was just more than she could handle dealing with at the moment. No sooner had she completed that thought than Ethel walked through the door from the back. Apparently while Elizabeth had been lost in her thoughts, Ethel had finished getting dressed and was now ready to leave.

As Elizabeth was checking her out and making her next appointment, Jake walked through the door. Elizabeth couldn't have been more stunned if she'd tried. Ethel thanked Elizabeth for the massage and turned to leave.

When she realized that Jake was there, she narrowed her eyes at the new arrival. With surprising vigor, she made her way over to him and snapped him on the head with her umbrella. Satisfied, she gave a sharp nod and walked out.

"That's for Elizabeth. Shame on you," she added as she pushed past him.

Elizabeth stood silent and guarded as she searched his eyes. Any hope she'd had that he was here to reconcile disappeared. His eyes were cold as ice. She'd seen that look many times but never directed at her, and it was like a knife to her soul. Defiantly, she lifted her chin a fraction.

"Lieutenant," she murmured, proud of her cool, crisp tone.

Her voice was steady. Mostly. Her eyes dry. Barely. Her heart...well, that was another matter entirely. That was breaking all over again seeing him here like this. Still, if he could appear to be okay, so could she. After all, he had to be acting, right?

"Can you explain to me why the hell I was just hit on the head by an old woman with an umbrella?" he ground out through his teeth.

"She's a little protective of me," Elizabeth edged.

"So you told her what happened and she's mad at me?" he questioned.

"No, Jake," Elizabeth sighed tiredly. "I didn't tell her anything actually, just that I screwed up. She convinced herself that you left me and apparently believes we should be together. Hitting you may be tempting but was all her idea."

Jake shook his head, jaw clenched. It didn't matter. Being smacked on the head by a little old lady was nothing to the pain that still filled his chest looking at Elizabeth right now. Even as angry, hurt and disillusioned as he was, she was still the most beautiful woman he had ever seen.

He could tell though that she hadn't been sleeping. Good, neither had he. The dark circles under her eyes gave her away and he wondered if he looked that bad too. In spite of everything that had happened, there was still some stupid, masochistic part of him that wanted to take her in his arms and make everything better.

Instead, he stiffened his spine and his resolve

and stalked across the small lobby. He took her hand and pulled it open and dropped the small silver piece of metal into her palm before folding her fingers closed around it. It had taken a couple weeks before he'd decided to give her back her key.

Elizabeth fought the tightness in her chest at his touch. There was nothing gentle in his fingers this time. The sharp edges of the metal cut into her palm and she welcomed the discomfort, hoping it would ease the emotional pain. No such luck though.

Without another word, Jake turned to make his way back across the street. Elizabeth's eyes filled despite herself and it took everything she had not to call out to him. She opened her fingers as he walked through the door, staring sightlessly at the small object that was evidence that the best part of her life was gone for good.

Elizabeth turned on her heel and tracked back to her desk. She threw the key dismissively on the piece of furniture then left the room. For now, she had other clients to see. She would cry later.

It was several hours later that she was ready to leave for the day. Business was good at least. Being busy kept her mind busy, which kept her from thinking.

Now, when her mind was free though, it would wander back to Jake and all the time they had spent together. The last few weeks especially were hard when she thought back to it. More than anything, she couldn't bear remembering that look on his face when he had walked away.

A heavy sigh passed her lips and she stood, grabbing her keys off her desk as she prepared to leave for the day. As she grabbed her purse, she heard a sound in the doorway. Katie stood there, looking at her almost hesitantly.

"What's up, Katie?" she asked, pasting a fake smile on her face as she looked at the younger woman.

"Fake smiles don't suit you, boss," she said gently, using the affectionate nickname she'd given Elizabeth when she'd started.

Elizabeth sighed.

"That obvious, is it?"

Katie nodded. "Did he leave?"

Elizabeth shook her head, "He's still there. I've seen him a couple of times, but – "

"Have you talked to him?"

"No, he pretended I wasn't even there. Today was the first time he's actually acknowledged my presence."

Katie knew some of what had happened that

day, but not all of it. She couldn't tell her all of it. It was just too much. Now, she searched her boss's face and decided she'd gone far enough for now.

"Well, the caterer just called and confirmed for the party on Christmas Eve."

"Okay, great. Thanks."

She waited, knowing that wasn't all that was on her friend's mind.

"You should try talking to him, you know. Maybe he'll listen now that he's had time to cool off."

"Katie," she began warningly, stopping when the other woman held up her hands in a gesture of surrender.

"Just saying."

"I know."

"Good night, Elizabeth."

"Night."

Elizabeth sat there long after Katie had left for the evening. She had thought several times about going to Jake and making him listen to her. More than anything, she wanted him back, even if only as a friend. She didn't know what to do though. He wouldn't even acknowledge her existence.

Katie didn't know the details of what had happened and that was the way it was going to stay. Jake didn't deserve to catch any backlash from anything that had happened. Elizabeth knew the current situation was all her fault and, while she would give anything to change it, she also knew there was nothing more to be done.

Her eyes fell on the key he'd brought to her earlier. That gesture in itself was more telling than almost anything else he could have done. Jake was gone. She had to accept that. Too bad she had no idea how to do it.

For so long, Jake had been there, the one constant force in her life. Without him, she felt lost. And there she was thinking about him again. Damn you, Jake, she swore silently. If he was cutting himself out of her life, the least he could do was cut himself out of her mind and heart as well.

It was hours later when she walked out the door, locking it behind her. Elizabeth sighed and glanced across the street where she had seen Jake's truck earlier. Somehow, knowing she was truly alone made it seem so much colder. It was going to be a long winter, she decided, climbing into her truck and driving away.

Jake sat in his small office at work, trying to force his mind to cooperate and complete the more mundane aspect of his duties. It wasn't all guts and glory. Someone had to do the paperwork. And, right now that someone was him. At least if they were out on a call, his mind would be occupied and he could stop thinking about Elizabeth.

He hadn't been able to get her out of his mind. Admittedly, he'd hoped that giving her back her key would somehow make it seem final enough that he could let it go. It hadn't.

Instead, he was staring off into space thinking about how exhausted and thin she'd looked. Rather than concentrating on the words staring at him from the computer screen, he was remembering how beautiful she'd still been. He was seeing again the unmistakable flash of pain in her eyes when she'd spotted him earlier. It had lasted only an instant before she'd masked it with a cool, mutinous look. Still, the anguish he'd seen in that one split second had matched the agony his own heart had been enduring. Despite everything, he'd had one hell of a struggle to not pull her into his arms and make everything better.

Cursing inwardly, Jake realized he'd been so lost in thought, he hadn't heard the tones go off in the station. Most of the crew had already rushed past his door and he hurried out to catch up to them. He could only hope to catch up on the situation as they drove.

The radio crackled and the dispatcher's voice came through, providing a little more detail.

"Two car MVC," she announced. "T-bone, blocking the road, believed to be with entrapment."

Jake responded appropriately and his mind raced, going through the protocol they would follow once on scene. The driver would stop the truck to block traffic and protect the scene. Then he would begin setting out the cones and everyone would scatter to their designated task.

Looking through the windshield, Jake could see the whole scene as they neared it. It was not going to be pretty. One car was almost completely demolished and no doubt would have to be cut apart to remove the occupant. He radioed that they were on scene as they approached.

The vehicle came to a stop and the crew hit the ground in motion. Within a minute, the scene had been secured. People in both vehicles were seriously injured so the officer on scene radioed for an additional ambulance as well as calling for an advanced life support unit.

Jake made his way to the car that had been hit in the side. As he walked he picked up enough pieces of conversation to gather that the woman driving the other car had been texting her boyfriend while driving. She hadn't seen that the light had been red and plowed straight through it and into the other car.

As usually happened in situations like these, it appeared that she was the least injured of everyone involved. She was, however, almost hysterical looking around at the damage she had done. Jake had to admit a lack of sympathy for her. With any luck, nobody would die as a result of her mistake as often happened, but hopefully she would never forget this. He hoped she would forever remember the consequences of her carelessness.

Battery cables were cut as the windshield was removed from the car. The driver's window was already gone but the door was crushed and would have to be cut off. Jake quickly donned a pair of latex gloves and climbed in through the back passenger door, the safest and quickest way to access the man sitting in the front passenger's seat.

The driver appeared mostly uninjured. Though somewhat dazed, he was conscious and lucid. Another paramedic worked to stabilize him and get him removed from the wreckage. He would be transported to the hospital as a precaution.

Jake turned his attention to the passenger in

the front seat. This man was groaning in pain, barely conscious. His face and torso were covered with blood. Jake introduced himself and the man turned to look at him.

His eyes widened slightly in recognition of one of his former co-workers. Robert Foster had been in the department years ago when Jake had first started. He'd helped teach Jake the ropes. Now, Jake was trying to rescue him from the mangled remains of a car.

"How've you been?" Jake asked with a forced lightness, as he gently covered the slightly older man with a blanket.

"I've been better," Robert said, with obvious effort. "How about you?"

"Better than you," Jake replied with a half-hearted chuckle.

He called over his shoulder for the brace to stabilize Robert's neck. Gently, he slid the rigid plastic in place, fastening it snugly to protect the man's spine. Outside, he could hear the machinery being started up and grabbed for the piece of cardboard that had been slipped into reach.

"It's bad isn't it, Jake?" Robert asked weakly.

"Well, you're not in the best shape, buddy, but you've got the best of the best here with you. You'll be fine."

The driver had been removed from the car already but it wasn't possible to get Robert out through there so they were going to have to cut him out. Jake calmly explained the process to the older man out of habit. He knew Robert already knew how things worked but old habits die hard.

Outside, the blocks had been placed to stabilize the car and the captain yelled in that they were going to begin cutting. Jake yelled back a response. He held the cardboard over Robert to protect him from any shrapnel that may have come flying as a result of the metal being cut away.

Conversation was almost impossible over the noise of the engines and screeching of the metal. Still, Jake spoke calmly to Robert about nothing in particular, his goal to keep the man alert and responsive. He silently urged the men outside to hurry as he felt Robert fading away. His breathing was shallow and his responses were becoming slower.

Jake's mind raced, trying to find a topic that would catch and keep the other man's attention long enough for his crew to complete their task. Nothing came to mind, so instead, he just tried to encourage the man to stay awake.

"So what's been going on with you?" he asked,

trying to keep it light while still speaking louder out of necessity. He wanted to keep the man's focus and also be heard over the racket just a couple feet away.

"Not much," Robert answered drowsily. "Heard you and Elizabeth finally got together, though. Always did think the two of you belonged together."

A lump formed in Jake's throat as he searched for an appropriate response. When he said nothing, the other man closed his eyes and sighed.

"But I also heard something happened and you're not together anymore. She messing around on you?"

Instantly, Jake went into defensive mode, "Of course not! Elizabeth would never do anything like that! Who told you that?"

Robert chuckled slightly, "Nobody told me. Just figured if you let each other get away, there must have been something pretty major."

Involuntarily, Jake clenched his jaw. Yeah it was pretty major, alright. Not that he could tell Robert the details. He wouldn't do that to Elizabeth. No matter what had happened, this was a small town still and some things were still deemed to be socially incorrect. Having a baby when you weren't married, or at least seriously involved, was one of those things.

"Listen to me, Jake," the older man whispered. "I've seen you two together. Nothing like it in the world, the way you kids look at each other. Love like that only comes along once in your life. Whatever it is, you have to work it out. Don't let her go. Promise me."

The old man's eyes glittered with unshed tears and Jake looked away, swallowing hard. Just at that moment, the last piece of the vehicle keeping Robert pinned inside was removed and Jake was saved from having to answer by the ensuing flurry of activity.

Within seconds, one of the paramedics on the scene brought over the backboard and it was slipped into position under Robert's backside. Carefully coordinating their movements, the crew was able to turn the man and get him into position without compromising his spine. Seconds later, he was loaded into the ambulance and Jake watched as it sped away toward the hospital.

# Chapter 11

Elizabeth pushed the cart through the small grocery store down the road from her apartment, halfheartedly eyeing the items on the shelves. None of it tempted her in the least. To be honest, not much did now. Jake would fuss at her. Well, he would have before. Damn, she had to find a way to get him out of her mind.

Just as she finished that thought, a gentle hand on her arm brought her back to the present. She almost flinched as her eyes met Laura's. For years, she had considered Jake's mother to be her own. To see her now, was almost more than she could bear.

The older woman's gaze bore none of the condemnation Elizabeth had expected. Had Jake told her of what had happened? Did she understand? Just not care? Or had he not told his family what she'd done?

Without a word, Laura folded her into a tight embrace. Elizabeth felt the hot sting of tears behind her eyes as she returned the hug. God, she missed them all. She hadn't dared show her face around their home though, only guessing at their reaction had Jake shared her revelation with the rest of his family.

When Laura pulled away, Elizabeth blinked hard. Damned if she'd cry now. She'd gone this long without doing so.

She should have known better though. Laura was just as observant as her sons. Her sharp eyes saw what Elizabeth tried to conceal.

"We miss you, kiddo," she said huskily, her own eyes a little brighter than normal.

"I miss you, too, mom," Elizabeth replied, sincerely.

She had long ago taken to calling her mom and Brad dad. God how she wanted to see them. In truth, she missed all of them: Brad, Laura, Nick, Logan, and of course Jake.

"How's Jake?" she finally asked, her voice cracking.

"Miserable, just like you," Laura answered, her tone was sympathetic. "I don't know what happened between you and Jake, honey. I don't need to know. That's between the two of you. But I hate seeing you both like this. You were so happy together. Are you sure you can't talk this out?"

"Some things can't be fixed, mom," Elizabeth murmured around the huge lump in her throat.

"I did something-" she paused, looking around

the store as she tried to find a way to explain without telling Laura exactly what had happened. "It can't be fixed now. It's too late. He won't even see me. God, if I could fix it I would. I'd give anything to take it back and make it better. I swear to you I never wanted to hurt him. I'd rather die."

Laura searched Elizabeth's face. The younger woman had been like a daughter to her for years. She knew the whole family missed her. Even Jake, whether he'd admit it or not. He had been surly and downright moody ever since the day he and Elizabeth had gone shopping.

No matter what anyone did though, he refused to talk about it. He seemed determined to get through it alone. Problem was, he didn't seem to be making any headway.

A few days later, Jake was at his parents' house, across from Elizabeth's practice, next to the fire station. He sat on the front porch watched Elizabeth drive away. Did she look even thinner or was it his imagination? Why was she there so late? He'd figured she would be long gone by then. That's why he hadn't hesitated to agree when his mother invited him for dinner. What difference did it make anyway? The back of a hand smacking his arm brought him back to the present and his brother looking back and forth between him and the retreating tail lights of the red SUV disappearing down the road.

Logan shook his head at his younger brother, "Man, why the hell don't you just go talk to her?"

Jake's expression turned to stone as he bluntly told his brother where he could stuff his suggestion.

Logan merely laughed. "Whatever it was, couldn't have been that bad man. Have you forgotten what Sharon put you through? And Ellie stayed right by your side. You screwed up with her a lot. I know. And she always stuck by you. So I have to wonder what in the world she could have done that's worse than what you did. She's one hell of a woman. Whatever you think she did, couldn't be worth letting her get away."

"You don't know what happened, so shut up," Jake growled irritably.

The older man raised a brow. "So enlighten me."

Jake sighed, warring with himself over whether or not to do just that. Logan would probably know what to do, he decided, or at least have some suggestions. He was actually kind of smart sometimes.

With another sigh, Jake accepted the cold beer his older brother handed him and began telling him the whole story. When he finished, Logan whistled long and low. It certainly hadn't been what he'd expected. He knew something had happened, but never knew what.

Jake was looking at him expectantly and Logan took a deep breath knowing his little brother was not going to like what he was going to say.

"Let me ask you something, Jake. Why do you think she told you? This was years ago. She could have taken this to her grave and you'd never have known the difference. Why would she put you both through this now?"

Jake thought for a moment, then shrugged. It didn't matter. She should have told him. She should have trusted him and let him make the decision on what to do with his own life. Logan watched his younger brother's internal struggle in silence for a moment then spoke again.

"She's right you know. You would have flipped out. You were going through enough as it was. Yes, she should have told you. But she did tell you. What did you do?" he asked pointedly.

Jake muttered something unintelligible under his breath, ashamed to admit that his brother was right. Elizabeth had tried to make things right. She knew where she wanted the relationship to go. He knew where he wanted it to go. If it was going to though, she wanted everything clear. And he'd walked away. He'd confirmed her fear and left her.

"Yes, it was wrong of her to keep it from you. But, think about this. Have you ever, since you met her, known Elizabeth to keep anything from anyone? Have you ever known her to deliberately hide things?

"It was wrong that she didn't tell you, but I think I can understand where she's coming from on this. That girl has always been crazy for you, Jake. You have to know that. Since you guys were kids, you've walked on water as far as she's concerned. She has always done anything and everything she could for you and I know you know that right here,"

With a serious expression, he jabbed a finger in Jake's chest.

"I think you also know right there, that you love her and that she loves you."

"But-"

"Hey, look," Logan cut him off. "I can't make any decisions for you. I know it hurts man. But does it hurt as bad as the thought of the rest of your life without her in it at all?"

Jake opened his mouth to reply, but found he couldn't. The thought of never seeing those laughing blue-green eyes again, never hearing her soft, sweet voice again, almost floored him. Still, he had to think about protecting his heart, didn't he? She had lied to him. How could he trust her again?

A small voice whispered that Logan was right and that Elizabeth had probably thought she was protecting him. Still, she had lied. Just like Sharon.

He sighed and went inside, no more sure of what to do than he had been before. His mother was in the kitchen, putting the finishing touches on dinner. An affectionate smile touched his lips, making him almost forget his agony for a moment. Almost. Then the smile fell away.

Without looking up, his mother nailed him.

"So are you going to talk to her?"

"Were you listening?" he asked, avoiding answering her.

She glanced at him before going back to what she was doing.

"No, but a mother knows when something is bothering her son. Not to mention that you two go from best friends to a lot more a few weeks ago. Then suddenly, she's gone. That alone is enough to tell me something's going on. You two have pretty much been joined at the hip lately so for her to disappear suddenly, is enough for me. So let's hear it," she demanded flatly.

"You wouldn't understand, mom," he muttered.

Laura merely gave him a look that spoke more eloquently than any words she could have uttered.

"I saw her the other day, you know."

Jake's head snapped up at his mother's words. He hadn't known that. Had Elizabeth told her what had happened? No, his mom would've told him so.

He struggled to resist the urge to ask her about Elizabeth. Had she looked ok? Was she still as beautiful as the last time he had seen her? Did she still love him?

Laura looked at her son and patted his hand again. Almost as if she could read his mind, she spoke.

"She's miserable and exhausted, looks like she's lost weight. And yes, she misses you."

"Are you sure? I mean, did she say that?"'

Laura chuckled indulgently, as only a mother can.

"She didn't have to, honey. You know, she takes full responsibility for everything that happened. Even now, she's looking out for you and your wishes. She wouldn't tell me what went on and blamed herself entirely. I told her she should try talking to you, but she didn't want to upset you more. You really should talk to her, dear."

She searched Jake's eyes for another moment in silence and, apparently satisfied with what she saw, she nodded.

"I want her here for Christmas. Nobody should spend Christmas alone."

Jake left a short while later. It was late but he couldn't sleep. He knew that. His mind wandered as he drove around aimlessly for a while. Somehow, he wasn't surprised when he ended up by the river.

It was his place to think. He and Elizabeth would often come here together. Sometimes, they'd picnic, sometimes talk. Other times, they were just content to sit next to each other and watch the sunset while the water flowed peacefully by.

Nobody would be there this late and it felt strange to be there alone. Somehow, it didn't bring him the soothing balm it usually did. He was just turning to leave when he heard a small voice in the wind.

Looking around, he saw a small form in the

snow, silhouetted by the moonlight. Years ago, Elizabeth had erected small crosses under the bridge, in memory of her parents. He should've remembered that it wasn't that far from here. He also should've remembered that she, too, came to this spot when she was troubled.

Jake knew he should leave but his curiosity held him rooted to the spot. The wind was fickle, carrying some of Elizabeth's words to him and drowning out others. In spite of himself, and calling himself ten kinds of a fool, Jake crept closer. He made sure to keep out of sight.

What he heard froze him where he stood. Her voice breaking occasionally, the words were obviously directed to her absent parents. His chest tightened as he listened.

"I don't know if you have much pull up there, but if you do, I could sure use your help. I messed up bad. You know, you always told me you do whatever it takes to protect the people you love and make them happy, no matter how much it hurts you. Well, I thought I was doing that, daddy. Really I did. I didn't tell Jake about the baby. I didn't want him to have to go through what I did."

Her face turned up toward the sky and he could see the moonlight reflecting off the trails of moisture that lined her cheeks.

"How could I tell him he lost a child? And now," her voice broke on a sob. "Now he knows and he hates me and I can't help him. I miss him so much, mama. I want to be there for him so badly, and I can't. And it hurts so much to know it's my fault he's hurting. Please mama and daddy, if you can, help him."

Jake had heard enough. His heart and mind full of what he'd just witnessed, he left as silently as he'd come. Climbing into his truck he just sat there for a moment. He couldn't get that last image out of his head.

Elizabeth on her knees in the snow crying, for herself but also for him. Her words replayed in his mind over and over as he drove. He'd been convinced before but now he was more certain than ever. He had to get her back.

Suddenly, he jammed his foot on the brakes, not the most clever idea on the snowy road, he admitted. His truck was able to handle it though and safely came to an almost stop on the shoulder, where he checked for any oncoming traffic. Seeing none, he forced the vehicle into a quick, tight U-turn and headed back in the direction he'd come.

Elizabeth's car was nowhere to be seen when he got there. Then again, he thought, he didn't recall seeing it before when he'd arrived either.

Had she walked? That didn't make sense.

He knew, though, that Elizabeth sometimes did things that didn't necessarily make sense to everyone else. Especially when she was upset, she preferred walking over driving. It didn't matter now, he thought though. He made his way down the icy embankment where he'd spotted Elizabeth awhile before, but she was gone. Damn, he swore. She must have gone home.

Hurrying back to his truck, he slipped a couple of times in the snow. Eventually, he made it back and clambered in. This time, he pointed it in the direction of their apartment complex. He drove far faster than he knew was safe. It didn't matter. He needed to talk to her.

Jake frowned as he pulled into the parking lot. There was no sign of Elizabeth or her car there either. Had he passed her? Had she gone somewhere else?

He paused for a moment, drumming his fingers on the wheel. Elizabeth was a safe driver so he was reasonably sure she'd not gotten into an accident, though a part of him urged him to check anyway. Maybe, she'd gone to Katie and Nick's.

A quick call to his brother would tell him, but he realized that it was way too late for him to call. He'd wake the kids and Nick would kill him if Katie didn't. That also meant Elizabeth wouldn't have gone there. With a sigh, he levered his lanky form out of the truck and made his way toward the stairs. He would just wait for her outside her door. She'd be back soon.

Elizabeth pulled her car into the parking lot. Somehow, she couldn't face going back to her empty apartment tonight. Knowing that Jake was so close and yet so far away was too much to deal with.

She'd decided to just sleep at the office. Carefully making her way down the darkened hallway, she pushed open the door to the first treatment room and lowered the table as far as it would go. At least that way if she fell off in the night, she wouldn't have far to go. She needed to set an alarm though since she had to work the next morning. Her phone usually pulled double duty as an alarm and she reached now to pull it out of her pocket, only to find it wasn't there.

A small puzzled frown marred her features as she tried to remember where she'd put it. She knew she'd had it earlier. Perhaps it was in her purse. A quick look through there dashed that hope as well. It must be still in her car then. That was the only other possibility. She hesitated for a moment, debating whether it was worth another trip outside to retrieve the device and decided it wasn't. There was a clock on the table in the room and that would suffice nicely.

Those tables were incredibly comfortable sometimes, certainly more than her big empty bed, that held only memories. Sweet, sweet memories. Memories of Jake loving her, holding her, making her laugh.

Jake listened to the ringing on the other end of the line. He had gone into his apartment about an hour ago and that had been after sitting outside for an hour waiting for Elizabeth to come home. The fourth ring sounded in his ear, followed by the soft sound of her voice. God, he missed hearing her voice.

Right now though, he needed to hear it in person not on the phone. He tried to tamp down the worry that was starting to gnaw at his gut. She was fine, he told himself as he gave up and went to bed. Most likely, she was angry at him and was ignoring his call. He would if he were her.

# Chapter 12

First thing the next morning, Jake called her again. It was still going to voice mail. Should he go corner her in the apartment? She'd have to listen to him then.

He darted out of his apartment and knocked on the door of hers. A couple minutes provided no answer and he strode to the rail to check the parking lot. Elizabeth's car was still noticeably absent. Had she stayed somewhere else last night? He tamped down the worry that reared its ugly head again. A quick call to his mom eased his mind though. Elizabeth was at the office. Evidently, she'd slept there last night instead of coming home. So the unanswered calls were a result of the issues between them, not her safety. Well, that at least, he could remedy.

Christmas was just a week away and he started formulating a plan in his head. He would need help though. Katie would be willing to help, he was sure. The hard part would be waiting the next few days to do it. If he didn't do it soon though, he was going to smack someone.

He was sick of everyone getting on his case about it.

Even Kyle had told him he needed to get it worked out. Only, he hadn't been so nice. Jake knew he deserved it though. It had been a couple days ago that his boss had taken him aside.

"Look Jake, I understand you guys have known each other forever. I know it's not easy. But you've got to get your ass together and get your head back into the game or you're going to get yourself killed, or someone else. You need to either work it out with her or get over it. Whatever you have to do. Just do it. Don't come back till you do. You have till the New Year."

The next morning, he called Katie. Her phone rang several times and he began to think she might not answer. When she did, her tone was quite brusque. His sister-in-law was none too happy with him he could tell, but there was nothing he could do about the past right now.

Quickly, he explained his situation and his plan and asked her if she could help. There was a long silence and he wondered if she would refuse. Instead, she asked him why she should help him.

"I messed up, Katie, but I want to make it right now. I need your help though. After the things I said and did, I can't just expect her to take me back. Even though she was wrong, there were things I said that I-" he paused. "I should never have said. Do you think she will even still talk to me if I do this?"

Katie paused for a second. Elizabeth had been so miserable in the last few weeks and there was no denying that. She knew her boss and friend missed Jake and needed him back in her life. As upset as she was, there was no doubt in her mind that Elizabeth would welcome Jake back with open arms. It may take a while but she would do it.

"Ok I'll help, but if you hurt her again," she warned.

"You have my word I won't," he promised.

It was almost eleven thirty when Elizabeth finally gave up pretending she was having fun. She found Katie and told her she was leaving. After giving her a heartfelt hug and a hearty "Merry Christmas," Katie shooed her out the door. If she didn't know better, Elizabeth might have thought the other woman was up to something, as eager as she had been to see her leave.

A few minutes later, she pulled up outside the apartment and got out of the SUV. It had started snowing again, and looked like it would be a white Christmas. She smiled, even as tears stung her eyelids. Her first Christmas since high school where she wouldn't even see Jake.

Her attention diverted, she slipped on a patch of ice and almost fell. She swore under her breath and walked more carefully over to the stairs. They really should clean the sidewalks better, she thought to herself as she climbed the steps, trying to ignore the small brown paper bag in the pocket of her coat.

She hadn't been feeling well lately. There had been a lot of stress she knew and was hoping that was all. A gut feeling told her there was something else though. There was only one other time she'd felt like this. So she'd stopped off at the pharmacy on her way home. Within a few minutes, she'd know if her hunch was right.

Fitting her key in the door, she sighed with a longing glance at the next door over. How she wished she could see him again, just for a moment. Instead, she whispered a Christmas wish to the closed door and entered her own apartment.

Moments later, Elizabeth was pacing in the confines of her small bathroom. The test would only take a couple minutes. Trying to control her anxiety, she couldn't help glancing at the little pink stick every time she passed it. Was it her imagination or was there another blue line showing up?

Finally the time was up. Taking a deep breath, Elizabeth picked up the wand. A sudden knock at the door startled her and she dropped it. She watched helplessly as the stick slid around in the sink and slipped into the drain.

It was just far enough that she might possibly be able to retrieve it herself. As she reached for it, another knock sounded. Who would be knocking on her door at midnight, Christmas Eve?

Then she shook her head, probably Katie coming to try to bring her holiday cheer. She grabbed her robe on the way out of her room, just throwing it around her shoulders and not bothering with the sash. This time she turned on the light as she made her way to the door. Katie knocked again and Elizabeth muttered under her breath.

She pulled the door open and the greeting froze on her lips. Jake, not Katie, stood on the other side of the door. Her fingers clutched the doorknob for support. It had to be her imagination. Some sort of daydream or something, it had to be her mind playing tricks on her. He couldn't be real.

"Jake," she whispered hoarsely.

"Hey, lady," he replied. "Um, can I come in?"

Too stunned to do anything else, she moved aside to let him in. After he was inside, she closed the door and stood there mutely, still trying to absorb the fact that he was there. She shivered a little, a belated reaction to the cold and he looked at her, his mouth going dry. The nightgown she wore shouldn't really even be called one. Or maybe it was just that he could see every inch of her in his mind and not in reality.

"You shouldn't have answered the door without seeing who it was," he admonished, his tone harsher than he intended and he winced when she stiffened slightly.

"I thought I knew who it was. I certainly wasn't expecting you."

"I know. Can we talk?"

She looked away, blinking fast, and he knew she was trying not to cry. He hated that he had made her cry at all, but couldn't bear the thought of her crying now. Not while he was standing just a few feet away. He reached for her and she drew back involuntarily, causing him to sigh again.

"Please. Don't cry. I'm so sorry, sweetheart,"

His words and gentle tone surprised her and she met his eyes. She couldn't read what was there but he didn't look angry like he had the last time she had seen him. God, this was confusing.

"What do you want?" she demanded.

"I, um, just needed to talk for a bit. I know I don't have any right to ask you to listen but please hear me out. I - " he paused for a moment, taking in her pallor. "Are you ok?"

Elizabeth looked away uneasily.

"Yeah, I'm just not feeling well. I've been stressed lately," she admitted pointedly.

"I know and I know it's because of me. That's why I'm here. I want to make things right. I miss you, Elizabeth. I miss your smile, your laugh, your kiss."

Elizabeth tightened the robe around her and looked at him uneasily. For the first time ever, she was wary of Jake. He'd made it abundantly clear that he wanted nothing more to do with her. Now he was here telling her he missed her.

Another wave of dizziness caught her and she wavered for a moment. Jake was instantly at her side reaching for her. Elizabeth put out her hand to keep him away. She still wasn't sure what was going on and Jake touching her was certainly not going to help the situation.

Jake sighed once more and took a step away. He really had done it, he supposed. Elizabeth didn't even want him to touch her.

"What can I do? Tell me please, Elizabeth. I need you back in my life."

Elizabeth closed her eyes against the sting of tears she could feel. God, she wanted so badly to run to him. She opened her eyes once more and met his gaze, searching for any sign of anger, the coldness that had been there so recently. Instead she saw only warmth and love, tinged with the pain of her absence.

She took a step closer and he held his arms out to her. Suddenly, she melted into his arms and he clutched her to him. He kissed her hair as her arms went around him.

"I swear I didn't mean to hurt you, Jake. I would never do that. I just thought – "

"Shhh," he whispered to her soothingly. "It's okay. I understand. I'm so sorry I wasn't there for you when you needed me, honey."

Elizabeth pulled away just far enough to meet his warm gaze. He tucked a stray lock of hair behind her ear, his touch as tender as she remembered it. Obviously, he wasn't mad at her anymore, and she knew she should be grateful, but she couldn't help but wonder what had changed.

Then she stopped thinking as his lips descended to cover hers. The warm, soft caress was the balm she needed to soothe her aching heart and she opened her mouth, inviting him in. He accepted the invitation without hesitation, kissing her slowly and thoroughly.

Several long moments later, he lifted his head and put a little space between them. As much as he wanted to continue kissing her, he knew they needed to talk. Taking her hand, he guided her to the couch and sat next to her facing her, still not relinquishing her hand.

"What happened?" she asked him, still confused.

He chuckled wryly. "Basically, everyone told me I was an idiot. They were right of course."

She was still confused, but nodded. His expression sobered and he spoke softly to her now.

"And I was there. The other night at the river," he added. "I heard what you said. I didn't want to stay and listen but I couldn't walk away. Now, I'm glad I stayed. What I heard finally got through to me."

"I see," Elizabeth murmured hesitantly, her face coloring in embarrassment. If he'd been there the whole time, he'd seen her break down. He'd heard her begging her parents to help. Of course, now it made sense. He was here out of pity. She stood and took a few steps away, needing the distance to clear her mind.

"So you felt sorry for me, Jake? Is that why you're here?"

"No! Not at all," he promised.

"I'm here because-" he broke off uncertain how else to explain his presence. "I tried calling you. Actually, I went back. That night. Just a few minutes after I left, I turned around and went back. But you were already gone. So I waited here outside your door. Then I tried calling. You didn't answer and never called me back."

"Yeah, I spent the night at the office. And I lost my phone."

He nodded, relieved that she hadn't just been avoiding him. That had been his biggest fear, he admitted to her now. It was hard to say, but the slight warming of her expression made it worth it.

"I didn't know what else to do, so I tried to make this big elaborate plan to win you back, and now, every word of what I planned to say has gone out the window. I have no idea where to start, Elizabeth. Help me, please."

"What would you have done if I hadn't let you in tonight?" she asked instead.

"Honestly? I probably would have broken down the door and made you listen. Or camped out on your doorstep till you came out again. I don't know. Whatever it took."

Elizabeth closed her eyes as sweet relief flooded her being. Jake stood and hesitantly walked to her, his hands gentle on her arms. When she opened her eyes once more, he touched her face gently.

"We still need to talk though," he said, taking her back to the couch. "Tell me what happened."

She bit her lip and started slowly. Before she knew it, all the pain she'd bottled up started pouring out. The entire time she spoke, he held her hands, occasionally releasing one or the other to wipe her tears.

She told him of finding out about the baby and how she'd actually gone to tell him, but when she'd gotten there, he'd been with the girl of the moment. He had seemed quite busy and she couldn't do it.

She told him of awakening in the night a couple days later with the horrible pains in her stomach, of finding her sheets soaked with blood. Sparing no detail, she told him of the trip to the emergency room. The agonizing wait had about driven her crazy. Then, she told him of the devastation when the doctor had told her she'd lost the baby.

When she finished, he looked around, feeling the unfamiliar sting of tears behind his own eyelids. In a way, he was glad she hadn't told him at the time after all. He knew he wouldn't have handled it the way he should have. Perversely, he also wished she had so he could have been there for her. He wondered aloud why she hadn't even told him when she had lost the baby, considering he wouldn't have been trapped anymore.

She took a deep breath, "After we made love that night, you apologized for it. You told me that it shouldn't have happened and that it didn't mean anything. That it was a mistake. How could I tell you that your 'mistake' was the best night of my life? And that sleeping with a girl you didn't actually want had created a child you didn't want? And then after that tell you that I had lost the child I hadn't even told you about?"

He nodded.

"I lied too, you know."

She locked at him confused.

"I did want you. I did think it was a mistake, but only because I was afraid to get involved with you that way. I was so afraid I'd hurt you. I had just gotten out of my marriage with Sharon and was so certain it was my fault. You had been there for me the whole time, doing everything you could to get me through. Even to the point of pissing me off enough to fight once, just to show that I still cared about anything. Do you remember that?"

She nodded and grinned. Deliberately picking a fight with him might not have been the best idea ever, but it had distracted him and gotten him to show some signs of life again. That had been her main goal. Dealing with his fury had been a minor price to pay for the victory and he'd forgiven her not long after.

"You had done all that for me, and I loved you for it. I was afraid of falling for you. I didn't realize I already had. And I was so afraid I'd hurt the one person who had done so much for me. I just didn't realize that in trying not to, I was in fact hurting you more."

"Wait? You love me?" she asked, incredulous.

"I love you. I want you. I need you, more than I've ever loved, wanted or needed anyone else. I talked to Logan about what happened and when he mentioned not having you in my life anymore, I felt like someone sucker punched me. I couldn't imagine my life without you in it."

Suddenly, she was in his lap, her arms tight around him. She was laughing and crying at the same time, and didn't care. Jake loved her. He wanted and needed her.

"I love you too, Jake," she whispered, cupping

his face lovingly with one small hand.

Jake reached up and covered her hand with his briefly, bringing it to his mouth for a kiss then lifting it away to look at it. Weaving his fingers through hers, he looked up into the eyes shining down at him. He knew now that, no matter what the circumstances were, he would have forgiven her even for this because to live without her simply wasn't possible.

"I came here tonight to talk about this but there was something else, too," he announced.

She tensed briefly and he almost laughed out loud. Instead, he reached into his pocket and pulled out the tiny box he'd stuffed in there before coming to see her. It was the same box he had checked and double checked and triple checked while he was pacing, waiting for midnight. He'd wanted to see her right at midnight. Katie had texted him just after eleven thirty to let him know that as he'd hoped, Elizabeth was on her way home.

He opened the box and the look on her face took his breath away. She smiled even as her eyes filled again. Then her eyes met his and he smiled too.

"Will you marry me, Elizabeth? I know I'm a pain in the ass and I'm stubborn and hard to deal with and-"

His words cut off as Elizabeth leaned down and kissed him into silence. Arms around each other, lips dancing together, it was a long time before either of them had a coherent thought again. When she lifted her head at last, he shifted uncomfortably, trying to make room for the hardness now aching between his legs.

"You talk too much," she announced after he had settled down again.

"Then how about this? Elizabeth, please be my wife. Make the rest of my life as happy as you've made it so far. Brighten my days and warm my nights. I can't give you everything you deserve but I can give you every bit of love I have."

Elizabeth bit her lip, one of the little habits that Jake had always found endearing. He could always tell when she was thinking or unsure of herself, because she'd nibble that lip. Now he reached up and kissed the lip free of the teeth holding it captive.

She had several little habits like that. When she was impatient, she bounced her leg. When she was angry, green sparks shot from her eyes and she pulled at her ear. When she was upset, she would play with her hair, sometimes just taking it down and putting it back up exactly the same way. Thinking of that, he reached up and tucked the lock of hair behind her ear.

"So what do you say?" he asked.

Elizabeth merely nodded, unable to speak around the lump in her throat. Her hand trembled slightly as Jake slid the ring on her third finger. It was a plain gold band adorned with a small, oval-shaped opal, surrounded by a circle of tiny diamonds sparkling with the fire of a thousand stars. It was, by no means, a traditional engagement ring.

With misty eyes, Elizabeth looked at Jake once more, "It's the one we saw when we were shopping. When you were getting your mom's necklace. How did you-?"

"I saw the way you looked at it. It wasn't a typical ring but very unique like you. Do you like it?"

Without a word, Elizabeth nodded. Then she sat up suddenly. She'd forgotten in the midst of everything else.

"Oh, before we...um..." she wasn't quite sure how to tell him.

She took him by the hand and led him down the hallway and through her bedroom. They continued into the small room where she had been when he knocked on the door. The stick she had dropped moments before was still where it had been and she reached for it now.

"I'm not really sure how to tell you so. I guess

273

I'll show you. I just found out," she chuckled nervously. "When you knocked it startled me and I dropped it. I would have told you. I just didn't know how to do it this time."

After a moment, she held the test out to Jake. He hesitated for a moment, not understanding. Slowly, he reached out and took it.

It took a moment for him to realize what he was holding. There was another moment still before the implication hit and the realization dawned on him. His gaze shot to hers, questioningly.

"Does this mean-?" he trailed off as she nodded. "You're going to have a baby? I'm going to be a father?"

Elizabeth nodded again and disbelief turned to joy. He grabbed her and squeezed her tight, kissing her hard. She squeaked and he released his hold slightly, setting her on her feet once more.

His hand lovingly cradled her face as he gazed at her in wonder. This was as it should have been all along. Elizabeth by his side, in his life, the mother of his unborn child. He leaned in to kiss her once more.

"Merry Christmas, my love," Jake whispered.

"Merry Christmas, Jake," she answered before being swept away again in the ocean of feeling that was Jake.

# Epilogue

Laura Carpenter blinked back tears of joy as she looked toward the back of the small church. New Year's day had dawned bright and cold and perfect for the wedding that had been hastily put together. Now, Jake and his brother were waiting at the front of the church for his bride-to-be.

The doors opened and Brad appeared, arm in arm with Elizabeth. She looked radiant in the ivory silk and lace gown she wore. Laura smiled broadly, remembering how shyly Elizabeth had asked if she could wear Laura's wedding gown to marry Jake.

It had easily been the best Christmas in recent memory for Laura. She'd found out they were getting married, that she was going to be a grandmother, and then the cherry on top had been the simple request from Elizabeth. Since Laura had no daughters of her own, she had been more than happy to pass the dress to Elizabeth.

She glanced over at her son now, who seemed completely oblivious to everyone and everything except the woman who was about to become his wife. His gaze trained on her to the exclusion of all else and she couldn't be sure but he seemed a little misty-eyed himself.

Elizabeth forced herself to take a steadying breath as she walked slowly down the aisle, arm in arm with Brad. Her gaze focused on the man waiting for her at the altar. Jake looked devastating in his black suit. His brother stood at his side, looking as sharp as ever, in his matching suit.

Laura's attention returned to the couple now making their way down the aisle and she smiled as Elizabeth made a detour to give her a big hug before taking her place in front of Jake. So many times through the years, she had hoped and prayed for this. She had always felt in her heart that the two of them were made for each other.

Jake swallowed a peculiar lump in his throat as his father approached with Elizabeth in tow. She looked absolutely stunning. The gown she wore was an off the shoulder dress. Its sweetheart bodice was snugly fitted and beaded with flowers. The skirt flared out from the waist and billowed down to the floor with a short train tailing behind her.

She wore a matching veil attached to the back of a tiara. Her hair was pinned up and back in a bun on top of her head, a few curls loose and framing her face. The little bit of makeup she wore, accentuated her eyes, making them seem even brighter than normal. Overall, the effect was breathtaking.

The pair approached the altar and paused for a moment, exchanging hugs and a kiss on the cheek. If he didn't know better, he would think his father actually a little teary. Brad gave him a stern look as he joined the couple's hands.

"You be good to her, boy," he instructed gruffly. Then he turned to Elizabeth and repeated his directive. "You be good to him, girl."

Elizabeth gave her word then turned toward the man of her dreams. Everything she had ever wanted was hers now. She and Jake repeated their vows, hand in hand and gazes locked.

It was the perfect day, the beginning of a new year, a new life together. Soon, they would welcome a new life into the world. For once, Elizabeth felt there really could be happy endings. This was hers, joined for life with her very best friend, her knight in shining armor, her Jake.